Hope Realized

Finding the Path to Sales Success

MARK A. THACKER

CONTENTS

ACKNOWLEDGMENTS

There were two common figures instrumental in the creation of *Hope Realized* and my first book, *Beyond the Mountaintop* – those two people were Bob Chenoweth and my wife, Pam. Both have gifts of writing and grammar that far exceed my abilities. It is simple to say, but also quite accurate, that both books could not have been written without their considerable help. Bob's major contribution to the story, including his words and overall storytelling expertise, far exceeds the credit he will receive. Bob and I have collaborated on many projects over the years; and his written words often are as I would have penned them myself . . . just better! Pam brings an expert editing eye, helping make my words sound as I meant them to sound. She was also a key contributor to elements of the story that help the reader feel as though they were in the diner themselves or were a party to key conversations. The three of us make a great writing team and I look forward to many more storytelling years.

I am also grateful to my children, daughter Stefani (and husband, Dan), son Kyle; and to my grandchildren, Keyden and Rio. While I enjoy the business roles of President and entrepreneur, they pale in comparison to the joy of being a father and grandfather. The titles of Dad and Papa make my life complete.

My thanks also extend to the rest of the Sales Xceleration corporate team: Chad Meyer, Maura Kautsky and Brandi Johnson. Chad – while I will be forever in your debt for your vision of what is now Sales Xceleration, I appreciate your honesty, integrity and deep faith so much more. Maura and Brandi – thank you for your creative vision, endless contributions to Sales Xceleration and your seamless entry into our company's servanthood culture. I also want to extend thanks to our 100+ sales management consulting Advisors throughout North America. It is their story, including their selfless attitude and strong desire to make a difference in the lives of business owners, that comes to life in the pages of this book. They are exceptionally strong sales leaders, but they are even better people.

CHAPTER ONE

The Detour

Steve was tired. Hungry, too.

And lost.

It had been another difficult week, and it was only Wednesday morning. He'd spent Monday and Tuesday upstate in meetings with two different clients, having dinner with the second client until 9:00 pm Tuesday. They were long-time clients. *Important* clients who had been key to the growth of his business – and would probably be essential to its future. But the meetings hadn't gone well. And now, adding insult to injury, he was forced onto an unfamiliar road by a detour.

After several miles, lost in thought, Steve also lost his bearings. Must've missed one of the signs, he thought, so he pulled off the road to check the GPS on his cell phone. It was then he noticed the phone's battery indicator at one percent. Like his own energy, the phone was depleted. Nearing zero. Behind the wheel, Steve's shoulders slumped and he groaned softly when he realized he had left the phone charger in the hotel room. He glanced again at his anemic phone. As if on cue, it powered down.

Steve surveyed the expanding farm fields along the road. If he could find his way, it would probably be easier to double back to the hotel – fifteen miles or so, he figured – than to find a store where he could buy a replacement charger. Or maybe he should just continue on with the dead phone and worry about it when he got home. No good options, really.

He continued on, the unfamiliar road beneath him snaking through a serene pastoral landscape he might have enjoyed if he hadn't been so focused on finding his way back to civilization.

What a day, he thought. *What a week. What a year!*

More miles unfolded, the road narrow and rough and hilly. Steve's fingers clinched the steering wheel in a white-knuckle grip. Breathe, he thought. *Just breathe.*

He again pulled the car to a stop beside the road, exhaled heavily and closed his eyes, trying to shut out the day, trying to block out his … situation. The deep breathing helped; and when he opened his eyes and returned to the road, he soon found himself at an intersection – a crossroad, really – but uncertain which way to turn.

Then he noticed something welcome, something hopeful.

Before him, like a veritable oasis, stood a diner. Its oversized sign was peeling and faded, but still revealed the diner's name to be *The Fork*. It was one of those old-time, aluminum-skinned, greasy spoon diners, the kind you see in black-and-white movies or nostalgic coffee table books.

Coffee, Steve thought. Sure, coffee might help. And maybe someone inside could tell him which way to go.

He pulled the car into an empty parking space near the front door and noticed a window sign. It radiated in bright orange neon: "Better pies, bigger pieces!"

Yes, indeed, Steve decided: coffee and maybe a light breakfast. Steve stepped from the car and opened the diner's front door. The aroma hit him instantly.

And pie. Even at this hour, definitely some pie.

CHAPTER TWO

The Questions

"Just sit anywhere, Darlin'."

Steve turned toward the voice. An aproned server stood behind the long counter, her back to him, facing the kitchen and gathering up an arm-length array of freshly plated food. She turned and nodded toward the empty booths. "Here, there, anywhere. I'll be right with you."

Steve surveyed the diner layout: four-person booths in the corners, "two-top" booths in between, a side room offering table-and-chair seating and connecting to another room in the back. There were padded stools at the counter, half filled with what Steve figured were regular patrons, drawn here like bees to a hive.

He walked toward one end of the diner and settled into a small booth, facing most of the interior space, his back to another man in the booth behind him. Surrounding Steve was the clatter and chatter of a thriving business, of happy customers having a good, perhaps even a great experience. Though his technology business was certainly not a restaurant, Steve remembered a time not long ago when his customers were satisfied and his employees engaged and happy.

"How ya doin'? Care for some coffee to get ya goin'?"

The server had already delivered the plates to a group of patrons in the side room and was now empty-handed except for an order pad in her left hand and a pen in her right. Her name badge identified her as Libby. Steve immediately thought she looked familiar.

"Coffee? Um, yes, that would be good. Black, please. No, wait, a little cream … maybe," said Steve.

"Sure thing. I'll bring it black," Libby replied. "If you decide on the cream, it's there on the table," she said, dashing toward the counter. "The menu's on the table, too."

They were right there, indeed, and Steve felt a rush of embarrassment for not getting his bearings more quickly. Then again, he seemed to have trouble grasping anything recently. The last few years had become an endless stream of distractions and disappointments, of false starts and failures. His confidence level, once fueled by being a respected innovator and market leader in a burgeoning tech industry, had run out of gas. Some days, most days lately, he wanted to stay in bed and pull the covers over his head. But that's not what business owners do. That's not what *leaders* do. Especially when success was expected – by customers and investors and employees. And their families.

His own family came to mind. Amy, his wife, would have already taken the younger kids, Braden and Abby to school this morning. Their older son, Seth, would have driven himself and his entourage to the high school. A born leader, that Seth. Charismatic, smart. Most people called him a chip off the old block, and that had always filled Steve with pride. Now it worried him. What if Seth followed in his footsteps too closely and lost his way, too?

Another worry. Another burden.

Steve sighed. He pulled out his cell phone to check in with Amy. The screen stayed black, the phone mockingly still dead.

"What'll it be, Sweetie?"

He looked up at Libby as she placed a steaming cup of coffee before him. Her smile was infectious, so he managed to return the courtesy.

Steve opened a menu. "I'm afraid I was a bit distracted," he said. "Lost in thought, you know. Lost in general, I suppose. What do you recommend – something light?"

"Saving room for pie, are we?" Libby asked.

"Maybe," Steve said. "Okay, probably."

"Hard to go wrong with the number 5," Libby motioned, and Steve nodded, accepting the recommendation without even finding it on the menu. He simply couldn't quite bring himself to be tasked with another decision right now, especially with so many others to be made.

Steve grabbed a small package of instant creamer from the tabletop bowl and started to open it, but then set it aside. Decisions. Questions. Dilemmas! Why did it always fall on him to have the answers? Yes, the company had taken off because he had made many smart moves early on. Or had he been merely lucky? That question haunted him now, for lately he couldn't seem to rise to new challenges.

He mulled over a laundry list of current, persistent problems, but merely recalling each one – and who knows how many he wasn't even remembering in the moment? – brought no clarity. And certainly no solutions.

He fiddled with his phone again, and then returned it to his pocket. It bothered him that he had grown so dependent on it to fill the void of quiet moments. Without the electronic distraction, he surveyed the diner's morning clientele: rural types, mostly, in groups of three or four, their voices rising and falling like an incomprehensible symphony. A few single patrons occupied the other two-tops, one sipping a soda with a folded newspaper in his other hand and commanding his attention; while the rest were invested in whatever glowed before them on their phones, as Steve would be, if only—

Sooner than expected, Libby set a plate on the table before him, saving him from the vortex of his thoughts. Actually, she set two plates down, bacon and scrambled eggs with cheese on the first, wheat toast on the second.

"Anything else, honey?"

"Hmmm? Oh, no, thanks, this'll be fine. Thank you."

Libby sat down across from him. She smiled in a way that said, "Talk to me," and for some reason Steve did. The floodgates opened and he told Libby about his business, its success, its recent challenges, and the burden he felt at not being able to simply snap his fingers and restore the company to the glory it once had. He told her about his family, too, and even about his key employees and their families. All depending on him. On him alone.

When he finished, the floodgates closing again with a heavy sigh, Libby patted his hand. "Sometimes it just helps to get it out, doesn't it, Sweetie? Sometimes that's an important first step."

Steve smiled, but lowered his gaze again to the tabletop, embarrassed that he just poured out his heart to someone he had met only fifteen minutes earlier. It was a sign of weakness, he thought, for his strength had always manifested itself by being in control, not asking for help, not *needing* to ask for help. Heck, he wouldn't even burden his wife with his problems. After all, why should Amy worry, too? Wasn't she practically running the family single-handedly, given that he was always working or away from home?

Steve looked back up at Libby. She nodded and winked, acknowledged the order-up bell from the cook, and then looked past Steve to the man sitting silently behind him. "Hey, Vance honey, what's that song number I like to play on the jukebox?"

"B-11," the man responded.

With that, Libby turned and yelled to a grizzled old gentleman next to the jukebox. "Jack, B-11 and a good swift kick."

Steve watched in wonder as Jack stood, poked at some buttons on the face of the jukebox, and then kicked it in a strategically dented place on the side of the machine. Instantly it clattered to life and the initial strains and refrains of "The Logical Song" by Supertramp engaged. A hit slightly before Steve's formative years, it had always been a favorite, and he found himself softly humming along as he ate his now-cold breakfast. But when the song took a quieter turn it also made Steve grow introspective.

It was true, he thought, that the questions can "run so deep for such a simple man."

CHAPTER THREE

The Nudge

Vance didn't mean to eavesdrop on Steve pouring out his heart to Libby, but he was in the next booth, and the story, so familiar, caught his ear.

Vance had met Steve before. Oh, maybe not *this* version of Steve, but others like him.

After a long career as a sales professional during which Vance could quickly get a read on a person and begin to zero in on their pain, he had encountered many other "Steves." Sure, they had different traits, both personal and professional, but they shared this in common: They had succeeded once – often spectacularly – and still had what it took to overcome unforeseen challenges and succeed again. That is, they could succeed again IF they could get out of their own way. And if they could quiet the deafening noise of the problems spinning in their heads. And if they could recognize they needed help, and ask for it, and have the guts to make hard decisions.

So many "ifs."

Most of the "Steves" Vance had encountered in his years as a sales management and Sales Leadership Consultant were brilliant in their particular field, and many, equally brilliant in starting a company. Trouble was, however, that they weren't gifted in every departmental discipline. Who among us is? Vance mused. He knew that a lack of experience in sales or finance or marketing often doesn't matter for the first few years of an organization's existence when momentum can fuel growth even in the face of rookie mistakes. But eventually, Vance knew, that lack of experience takes its toll.

From the story he had overheard, that certainly seemed to describe *this* Steve as well. And though he seemed to be at or near what Vance considered the first critical phase of saving his business – accepting the reality of the situation – he might not necessarily be ready for the all-important next phase: actually admitting he doesn't have all the answers anymore and that he needs to ask for help.

Certainly, getting the help you need can sometimes take a nudge and an offer. And that's why, when Steve stepped away from the table to go to the restroom, Vance had left him the note, tented between the tines of a fresh fork:

> *In life and in business there are many forks and many roads. You will always have challenges, but you will always have choices and opportunities, too. Your first choice is to decide where you want to go. If success is your answer, you must decide what success looks like, because you can't reach a destination you can't envision.*
>
> *Meet me here next week, same day, same time. Till then, think about what I've said. Define the success you seek. Be specific. Focus on the revenue you need. If you can do that, I am confident I can help you find the path to success.*
>
> *Vance*

Vance couldn't yet determine whether Steve was the type of man whose pride would get in the way of accepting help, let alone paying for that help on the professional level under which Vance served his clients. Sadly, Vance had seen too often that many business owners wait too long to ask for help – or never ask at all, losing their businesses when there was another option. Rather, they cling to a shaky legacy of past and diminishing successes and can't let go of their stubborn pride long enough to understand what Vance considered the greatest business success lesson:

> *The greatest sign of wisdom is recognizing you need help.*
> *The greatest sign of strength is asking for the help you need.*
> *And the greatest sign of leadership is accepting help when it is given.*

Given.

There was that word again.

Given.

It took root in Vance's head. He tried to dismiss it. Tried to dismiss this rapidly gestating wild idea. Giving away the help he normally charged for? Crazy, he thought. After all, he prided himself on being a sought-after professional, someone whose insights, solutions, and business-saving wisdom were recognized and rightfully rewarded. After 25+ years in the corporate world, he had earned his position of respect, and he knew his sales management services were valuable and worth every penny. So why did the idea of *giving* his services to Steve even enter his mind?

Still, it was there. And behind that impulse Vance could see a vision of Charlie, standing there with a big grin on his face.

Ah, yes, Charlie. His old mentor. Nudging him with the notion of giving and reminding him that Vance had once been like Steve. Doubting his own value, even though he had been a huge success not long before. Doubting that others would pay for the wisdom he had accumulated. Doubting he would be listened to again like he had been in the past.

Vance smiled at the thought, at the memory of how, with Charlie's help, he had overcome where he had once been in his own journey, drowning in the quicksand of doubt and denial. It had been a remarkably easy mindset to fall into. After all, he had reached a level on the corporate ladder where his hard work and dedication had been rewarded time and again until he found himself at the VP level. But after many years at that level, change was afoot as it always was, and even though he had seen the proverbial writing on the wall, it still hit him like a sucker punch when the merger happened, when the downsizing came, when the axe fell. He had been part of the team that thinned the herd during the merger, and when it was nearly done, he found himself among those who were laid off.

Just like that.

And there he was, licking his wounds and wandering aimless in a fog, wanting *back in* but not really wanting to be there at all. Stuck in the notion that corporate life was all he knew. Such was his mindset until he had bumped into Charlie that fateful day years earlier at The Fork.

Yes, Charlie. Such a marvel, that man.

The connection between Vance and Charlie had been easily forged because their paths had been similar. Charlie was smart, creative, personable, and had also ridden a wave of one success after another up the corporate ladder. His time was mainly spent with one company because that was the way of the corporate world back then. But change ultimately is an irresistible force and the corporate growth Charlie had helped build eventually overtook him. Whereas Vance could have seen the axe falling if he had dared to look, Charlie had truly been blindsided. He had thought his position as VP of Sales was as secure as any in the organization. Until it wasn't. Until he was out the door.

Vance had been intrigued as he listened to Charlie that day. He had been sinking deeper into the self-doubt that could have consumed him and defined the rest of his days, but Charlie was there with a lifeline Vance hadn't even realized he was grasping for.

Charlie's story *was* that lifeline. Not the story of his downfall, but the story of his ascendency. Of how he had taken stock of his attributes and talents. Of how he had listened to his inner voice that told him the corporate world was no longer his home. Of how he had recognized a need – a deep and abiding need – that smaller companies had for his experience, his expertise, his knowledge. His wisdom. The lifeline was Charlie's story of how he had taken a leap of faith – in himself.

In fact, years earlier Charlie had reinvented himself at 59 years old and found not only new heights of success, but also his calling. He had discovered his purpose. In the process, he told Vance that day, he wasn't merely making a living; he *was living!*

As Vance continued to navigate the now familiar detours away from The Fork, he had an unshakeable urge to call his old mentor. To thank him again for turning Vance onto a similar path – the path of helping small to mid-size businesses and business owners in need. Vance wanted only to hear Charlie's voice, to listen and learn still more from this wise man.

But Charlie was gone. Just two weeks earlier the disease had taken him with merciful swiftness. Vance felt emotion rising within him. Even so, he smiled at the memory of the memorial service and how the room had been filled not only with Charlie's friends and family, but also with business owners for whom Charlie had made such a difference. Such a giving person, they all said.

Giving.

There it was again. That notion. That not-so-gentle nudge from Charlie.

Vance stopped the car at a red light. By the time it turned green, he had made the decision. He would pay it forward. In honor of Charlie, he would find a way to help Steve.

If Steve would let him, of course.

CHAPTER FOUR

Three Messages

Steve sat outside the diner in the idling car. Libby had given him directions for getting back to the highway and had even given him a whole fresh-baked apple pie "on the house" if he promised to come back.

He did promise to return, his next visit already in his mind for several reasons: kind-hearted Libby, the delicious food, the atmosphere that harkened back to the simpler days of his youth. The jukebox. The music. The pie.

And the note.

Steve looked again at Vance's message. It was written on the back of the bill, and Vance had taken care of that, too, paying it covertly and slipping out unnoticed. Like Libby's free pie, it was a kindness that Steve found surprising, humbling, and a little embarrassing. Did he appear to need help that badly?

As Steve sat in the parking lot watching people come and go, he wondered if his own attitude was part of the problem. Did he project to others that he was frustrated and desperate? Hopeless, even? And if so, were his clients reluctant to renew their commitment to a company on the ropes, let alone put faith in a man who seemed to have no faith in himself? He thought he was hiding all those emotions well, but perhaps he wasn't.

It was a bit of an epiphany for Steve. Unfortunately, that revelation brought no easy answers; nor did it bring instant solutions to the many problems plaguing him and his company.

He looked up at the neon sign in the window. *Better pies. Bigger pieces.* That's what his business needed, Steve thought: his company's version of a new and improved pie and a bigger piece of it. Another epiphany, Steve mused.

His phone buzzed, pulling him from his reverie. The phone had been brought back to life because "Jukebox" Jack – an old guy who looked anything but tech-savvy – had produced a compatible charger and let Steve borrow it long enough to charge it back up halfway. Steve tapped the phone and discovered three missed messages, two from work and now the new one from Amy. The work-related messages were more of the same: another client was threatening to move to the competition, and there was an RFP due by morning that needed his urgent attention. *Why couldn't anyone else handle these problems? Why do I always have to be involved?* And from Amy: *Seth has a swim meet tonight, final one of the season. Will u be home in time to make it?*

That last message gutted him. He knew there was no way he could be there for the swim meet. It was, yet again, another missed family commitment. He wanted nothing more than to be there for Seth, to see the surprise on his son's face when he actually showed up for once. But Steve knew he really had no choice. The RFP had to get done and he was the only one who could see it through to completion. And who knew, maybe *this* RFP would be the turning point, landing a new client that could provide the revenue to help turn everything around. Maybe. Probably not, he conceded. But maybe.

Steve texted Amy: *So sorry. Again. Not looking good. Will be home late. Will u record Seth's events and send so I can watch later? Heading to office now. Bringing pie home. Love u all. Really sorry.*

Steve sighed and put down the phone. After a few deep breaths, he pulled Vance's note from his pocket again:

> *In life and in business there are many forks and many roads. You will always have challenges, but you will always have choices and opportunities, too. Your first choice is to decide <u>where</u> you want to go... If success is your answer, you must first decide what success looks like, because you can't reach a destination you can't envision.*

Challenges. Choices. Opportunities.

And success? What measure of success could be more important than simply spending more time with his family? More quality time was coveted, sure, but also more *quantity*.

Again, Vance's note:

I am confident I can help you find the path to success.

Steve knew right then that he would come back to The Fork in one week. That he *must* come back. After all, he had promised Libby he would return, he owed Vance a breakfast, and he owed it to his family to seek an answer, to seek solutions. To seek a return to success.

But before he started back to the office, he programmed the diner's location into the GPS on his phone. He wanted to be sure he could find his way back to this crossroad far from the beaten path.

CHAPTER FIVE

Choices At The Fork

The week went by as most weeks did for Steve, with many challenges big and small, most just a different version of the same problems he had been experiencing for the last couple of years. He felt fortunate for one thing, at least: his key staff members were, so far, sticking with him. But for how long? After all, they had to know the position the company was in and where things were headed. Didn't they? Or were they like he had been for too long, ignoring the obvious because it wasn't a pleasant reality?

What his team didn't yet know was that Steve had stumbled into a glimmer of hope and had quietly found himself looking forward to returning to The Fork -- out of curiosity, if nothing else. So, he had cleared his calendar and when the day came, *this day*, he started out early, following the GPS on his fully charged phone, turn by turn.

During his drive, Steve's mind kept wandering back and forth between the anticipation of his meeting with Vance and that night when he had worked on the RFP late into the evening alongside his Project Engineer Lorenzo and one of his sales reps, Joe. They were on autopilot, exhausted and going line-by-line, often drawing from past failed RFP responses, as they populated the information required to submit *this* RFP. Lately, they'd had a habit of filling out any RFP that was sent to them, hoping they might win one even if it didn't seem like a good fit. This was one of those opportunities unlikely to be won and they all seemed to know it. So, with no real confidence in the outcome, it seemed obvious to Steve that none of them had any enthusiasm to invest in the process. Still, they muddled through and had it ready to send just before the deadline.

The house was mostly dark when Steve had finally made it home, the kids in bed and Amy probably upstairs reading and ready to turn in. Because his phone had died again late in the day, Steve had not seen any videos or photos Amy might have sent from the swim meet. So, he located the extra charger he kept in his home office and started powering up the phone. While it charged, he checked his messages. A prescription was ready for pickup at the pharmacy, his cell carrier confirmed the success of his monthly automatic payment, and Amy had indeed sent several messages, all with photos or videos from the swim meet.

He was just starting to watch the first video when Amy came into his office and wrapped her arms around him from behind. Steve paused the video and leaned into her embrace.

"Pie," she had whispered into his ear. "You promised pie."

Moments later, they stood at the island in the kitchen, Amy gushing over the pie and talking about the meet – Seth won the butterfly, placed second in the backstroke, and the team had fallen just short of the win in the relay. She showed him the full set of pictures she had taken at the event, of the boys standing around and cheering on their teammates, of Seth in action in the water, and after the meet was done, Seth wearing his medals, flanked by his family. Except for Steve.

They had made small talk about their days, then, with Amy telling him about her photography class, playing taxi-mom for the kids, and attending the Homeowner's Association meeting. Steve knew it was his turn to talk about his day, but lately, he didn't like talking about his work. All it did was make him think about his business, when in reality, he wanted to escape work and just be with his family. He knew Amy asked because she cared about him, but it was hard to find the balance between not shutting her down and drudging up the day he wanted to forget. Steve shared a little about the RFP and the business of the day. And then he told her about the detour and the diner, because this was the one part of his day that was hopeful. He hadn't gone into detail or told her of his plan to return to The Fork, for it was late, and he was at a loss to truly understand, let alone explain, his compulsion to pay another visit to that eatery in the middle of nowhere.

Now, as Steve got closer to the diner, he noticed something: the detour signs were gone. This was no longer an alternate route, but rather it was now a route that enabled him to go straight to where he was supposed to go.

He arrived early and immediately sucked in the aroma of fresh brewed coffee and pies that might still be baking in the back. Libby was in the side room refilling coffee, but he could hear her voice, brimming with authentic and perhaps perpetual delight. Steve had a flash of thought that maybe his life would be easier and his demeanor cheerier, too, if he had chosen a different career path.

Steve seated himself in the booth Vance had occupied previously but was careful to take the opposite seat in case Vance was a stickler for his favorite spot. He checked his notebook, going over the brief notes he had entered in preparation for today. His notes attempted to answer the big and frustratingly complicated questions Vance had posed outright or suggested in his note: What was success? What revenue would it take to restore the company to profitability? Where did he want to take the company? What would this new level of revenue provide him that he doesn't have today? And on and on. He closed his eyes for a moment, hoping to quiet the noise of the diner and find focus.

"You came back!"

Steve opened his eyes and looked up. Vance stood beside the table, hand extended. Steve started to rise, but Vance motioned for him to remain seated. They shook hands across the table and Vance flashed a smile. "Nice table choice," he said.

"Thought maybe it was *your* spot," Steve responded.

Vance chuckled. "Guilty as charged. I like sitting here because I have a full view of what's going on. It helps to be able to take everything in and not get lost in a view that's too close at hand."

Libby sidled up to the table. "Look what the cat dragged back in! Glad to see you both. Coffee all around…" she said, already pouring, "and I'll give you a few minutes before I pester you again."

Even as Libby spoke, Steve was studying Vance. The man across the table was a bit older, maybe mid-fifties. Before he had taken his seat, Steve had noticed that Vance was shorter than him, but also that he had *stature,* a confidence in his bearing. Vance had an easy smile, too, sincere and personable. He seemed instantly likeable. Genuine.

Vance glanced quickly at the menu and then placed it back on the table. "I know this thing by heart," he said. "Today seems like a day for the Starter Platter."

Steve found the item on the menu. He nodded. "Looks good," he said, and he, too, placed the menu face down on the table.

The two men locked eyes.

Vance's eyes widened and he grinned. "What if I had said the goose liver omelet with a mayonnaise and mustard drizzle sounded good, Steve? Would you have gone along with that?"

"Excuse me?"

Vance leaned in. "Last week I couldn't help overhearing that you accepted Libby's menu suggestion without pause. Today you followed my lead just as quickly. Why is that?"

Steve looked away, then met Vance's eyes again. "I don't know. I guess there's just so many choices on the menu that it helped to narrow it down, that's all."

Vance sat back again. "Steve, if you'll forgive me for being blunt... From where I sit, it seems like you welcome any opportunity to avoid considering the possibilities. You seem to relish the chance to make an easy decision when you can – or perhaps to avoid making a more complicated one. Oh, I know it's a trivial matter, ignoring the many menu choices at The Fork, but I wonder if this minor behavior isn't in some way insightful about the way you approach your business."

He continued: "You know, Steve, there's an old story, an urban legend perhaps, about James Cash Penney..."

"The founder of the JC Penney stores?"

"The very same. The story goes that Mr. Penney was meeting a candidate for an important position in his company and met the man for lunch. As soon as the food arrived, the man salted his food before tasting it. Right then Mr. Penney knew the man would not be a good fit for his company. After all, shouldn't a person assess the situation before deciding what will make it better?"

Steve smiled. "Point taken," he said. "I've heard the same story, although I heard it was Edison who did that."

Vance nodded. "Edison, too, perhaps. Or maybe it was Henry Ford. Or General MacArthur. The story might be a fable, but the lesson remains valid. It's about leadership, of course, but it's also about awareness and decision-making."

Libby returned: "So, gentlemen, what'll it be? What's your decision?"

Steve opened the menu again. "I may need just a bit more time. Unless, of course, you have a goose liver omelet with a mayonnaise and mustard drizzle."

CHAPTER SIX

Another Path

After surveying the full menu, Steve still opted for the Starter Platter. "It's really what I want today," he told Vance. It'll give me a chance to sample several things and discover the best choices."

"Fair enough," Vance conceded.

They spent the next fifteen minutes sipping the hot coffee and sharing personal and professional background information. Vance began, telling Steve that his last corporate role had been ten years earlier, at which time he had been "downsized" at what seemed like the worst possible time, with two kids in college and a new home being built, not far from the diner. Before he engaged in the next chapter in his life – his *current* chapter – as a sales management consultant, he had taken the classical route through sales: started "carrying a bag" in his twenties (fresh out of college) and then progressed to a District Manager, Regional Manager and then VP of Sales for the final 15 years of his corporate career.

After the initial "glamour" of being a jet-setting company mover and shaker (top performer, he admitted) wore off, Vance had grown increasingly tired and resentful of travelling so much – four days each week, three weeks each month – which forced him to feel disconnected from his family. He admitted to missing out on many key events in his children's lives.

He admitted to leaving the burden of raising the family to his wife, who also worked hard serving others in a job she loved. And he admitted to putting career success before success at home.

Vance then stated, "I kept telling myself all these sacrifices were for the betterment of the family, but in reality, the sacrifices were more about my personal success. Oh, there isn't any doubt that I wanted to provide a better life for my wife and kids – but a promotion, more money and prestige, and being in charge of more revenue and people … those things were the real lure."

Steve looked down at the gray and yellow mid-Century-patterned Formica tabletop and then stared into his coffee, but Vance had continued: "I also came to resent the fact that the corporate higher-ups often didn't listen to me about what needed to be done. I had all this knowledge, you might even call it wisdom, I guess, but they wouldn't listen anymore. I had gray hair by then but limited control. I couldn't understand why, as the person in the organization who arguably knew more about sales than anyone else, I wasn't often listened to when considering a sales path for the company."

Vance sighed and leaned in closer to Steve again. "After I got let go, and I finally had the time to step back and take a higher-level view of my life, I realized I had regrets. Deep regrets. About the choices I had made. About choosing work over family. About continually rationalizing that I was the one making the sacrifices; and not realizing that my family had made bigger sacrifices than I ever could.

"Steve, when the moment came and I was no longer VP of Sales in that rat race, I had two choices. I could venture back into the jungle and try to land something similar – essentially forcing myself back into a corporate culture I had grown to despise – or I could seek another path."

Libby delivered the food, asked if they were "all good," and rushed off to answer another food-ready-on-the-counter bell. Steve began eating his breakfast – unsalted – as Vance continued his story. He listened intently as Vance told him about Charlie, and how Charlie had helped him discover for himself what had given Charlie joy in his life, too – helping others. He listened as Vance recounted how Charlie had illuminated an option where he could help others while using his hard-earned experience and expertise and wisdom: consulting for small to mid-size businesses in need of sales and leadership guidance.

"I'm really fortunate that Charlie took me under his wing and opened my eyes," Vance said. "Not only do I now have more control and a greatly improved work/life balance; and not only do I feel important and valued again – I feel like I'm making a real difference these days, because now I also have the opportunity to help these business owners and leaders take back portions of their own lives. Like Charlie was for me, you might say I'm a pathfinder, helping people like you, Steve, identify, illuminate and navigate pathways to new levels of success." He paused a moment, as if reflecting on his journey. "Steve, I went from dreading what the next business day had for me to waking up excited by the opportunity to help make other people successful and happy. I guess I lead a pretty fulfilling life these days."

Vance smiled and picked up his fork. "Enough about me. Tell me the Steve story."

Steve took a sip from his coffee mug and sat back against the time-worn red vinyl seat, looking Vance square in the eyes. He spoke first about his family and said he understood how Vance had felt about priorities and sacrifices. He showed Vance a photo on his phone, of his family – without him in the picture.

Steve told Vance he had recently turned 50, and that he had been a "technologist" who was experienced in software development. He told him about how he had been an in-the-trenches software geek earlier in his career, jumping from one company to the next because he was in high demand. Eventually, he told Vance, he had privately developed a software platform that helps manufacturing businesses bring down costs and speed up existing processes, thus enabling fulfillment of new opportunities. He described the system as having been revolutionary when first developed and how it helped companies control cost and inventory, escalate operational efficiency, and result in quicker time-to-market.

His skill set, Steve admitted, was in the creative tech side of things, but he had soon found himself forming and owning and attempting to lead a company that quickly took off despite his leadership inadequacies. He confessed to not having given much thought to the importance of developing leadership skills along the way, but now he knew he should have honed what limited skills he had whenever he had the chance.

As time went on and competitors stepped up their game, Steve said, his company started losing ground. At first it was almost a blessing that the business slowed a bit because the company had been hard pressed to meet demand. But soon enough that relief became cause for concern, and now the company was bleeding. Badly. All the companies that once had found him due to his state-of-the-art software now didn't reach out very often.

"And you're right," Steve admitted. "Nowadays I guess I'm just looking for any way to make easier decisions."

"Well," Vance said, wiping the corner of his mouth with a napkin, "I can't promise to deliver easy answers, but I'm certain I can help you see your choices more clearly so you can have more confidence moving forward."

Steve took a moment before responding, "Yes, Vance, I would very much appreciate your help. If I can afford it, that is."

"I'm pretty sure you can," Vance replied. "Let's just take the first step."

CHAPTER SEVEN

The Right Questions

Libby cleared the dishes, refilled their coffee mugs, and disappeared in a flash.

"For as cheery and chatty as that woman can be sometimes," Vance said, "she can also dash in and out like a cat. She has an innate sense of when to become part of a conversation and when her involvement would be a distraction."

Steve cocked his head slightly. "Why do I think you are making a point for me with that observation?"

Vance laughed. "You're on to me already, aren't you? Okay, I confess… Sometimes I see parallels in the moment that, for me at least, bring clarity to a problem." He blew lightly across the top of his coffee, trying to cool it a bit, then placed the cup back on the tabletop. "What occurred to me when I made that observation about Libby is the connection to the particular traits of a good leader: it seems to me that a good leader knows when to intercede and when to stay in the shadows. They know when to step in and become a catalyst for productive problem solving, but they also know when stepping in would simply add stress and complicate team problem solving that is already starting to gain traction."

Steve cleared his throat. "I'm not sure I have that innate sense, as you called it, to be, well, I guess the word would be *discerning*. Or maybe it's about wisdom or judgment…"

"It's all part of the leadership equation, Steve. Ultimately, if you don't feel confident knowing when you should insert yourself into a situation, ask yourself what your team has to gain by your involvement."

Steve's eyes brightened a bit. "It sounds like what you are saying, Vance, is that sometimes leadership is about staying out of the way."

"Exactly!" Vance responded. "Congratulations! That was a big revelation for me earlier in my career, but it's been critical to my success and the success of those around me."

"But it's not just about knowing when to stay out of problem solving, right?" Steve replied. "And it seems like it's not about constantly stepping in with all the answers either. Isn't it also about knowing *how* to help others stimulate solutions on their own?"

Vance nodded. "Right again. And what do you suppose is the best tool in your arsenal for stimulating creative solutions?"

"Well," Steve began, "I know that simply staying out of the situation can be appropriate at times, but I suppose solutions could also be easier to see clearly if the right questions are asked." He smiled and shook his head from side to side. "Kind of like how you just asked me a question and it helped me arrive at my own understanding, right?"

Vance grinned approvingly. "To quote a wise woman named Oprah, 'Ask the right questions and the answers will always reveal themselves.'"

Steve shook his head. "That sounds a little too simple. I'm not sure I am hard-wired to recognize and ask the right questions."

Vance reached into his pocket and pulled out his wallet. From the wallet, he dug out a small card. "Another quote," he said, and then began reading the text on the card. "If I had an hour to solve a problem and my life depended on the solution, I would spend the first 55 minutes determining the proper question to ask, for once I know the proper question, I could solve the problem in less than 5 minutes."

"More Oprah? Steve asked.

"Someone almost as wise," Vance said. "Einstein this time."

Steve chuckled, then grew serious again. "I don't know, Vance; the big question that is already irritating me is, 'How do I find within myself that all-important proper question Einstein spoke of?'"

"Relax," Vance said. "Once you get the hang of leading with questions instead of stressing over having all the answers, it gets easier." He raised his cup again and sipped the coffee, and then said, "As I see it – and again, this is something I learned from Charlie – if you feel stuck you can always lead with one of these questions: 'What if?', 'Why not?', and perhaps most important of all, 'What do *you* think?'" He waited until Steve locked eyes with him again. "Ask that last one of your team members and you may find out that the answers, the *solutions*, are lurking just beneath the surface."

Seconds later, it began to rain, the raindrops streaking down the window beside the booth in fluid furrows on the field of glass. Both men noticed the rain and watched it for a few moments, as if the percussive patter of the rain drops on the window were a natural overture leading into the heart of the discussion.

"So, Steve," Vance began, breaking the silence, "if we agree that the right solutions begin with asking the right questions, that brings me back to those key questions I wrote on the note last week. The first question, the *most important* question, I have for you is, 'What does success look like to you?'. Have you thought about that?"

"I have," Steve said. He pulled his notebook onto the tabletop and flipped through to a dog-eared page.

"And what did you come up with?"

"Well," Steve began, "I think if I could just hire a really good salesperson to fill the void in my current sales team and find us some new accounts, it would sure take the financial burden off of me, as well as allow me not to travel as much. I just haven't been able to identify the right person. I have had a few people, but nobody worked out – that is why I have been on the road so much. It would also be helpful to have a really competent Sales Engineer that could handle the RFPs and sales operations, so I don't have to be involved in every transaction."

Steve continued down the same path for a while and Vance allowed him to go on. He had learned that business owners typically move straight to "fixing" the problem before determining their destination. They tended to choose routes and their modes of transportation before they could even tell where they are travelling to.

As Steve talked, his eyes remained focused on the notebook before him, reading his notes verbatim. When he finally looked up, Vance held up his hand to stop him before he went any further.

"What I really want to know, Steve, is this: If we are meeting in this same booth one year from now and you share with me that your life is amazing, what does your life look like? How has it changed? How do you feel? How has your personal life been positively impacted? What does your business look like – from a big-picture perspective, I mean – not a description of who is working there and what role are they playing? Do you see the difference? If you need to, just close your eyes and imagine what a year from now feels like when things have turned around and you are enjoying your success."

Steve's face flushed. "Sorry," he said, embarrassed by going on so long sharing information that wasn't even what Vance wanted to know. This wasn't the start he was hoping for.

"It's okay, Steve," Vance reassured him. "You are merely overthinking this. That's common, but premature. Before we can help you get where you want to be, we need to define that destination, right?"

Steve nodded, his face still warm from his misstep.

"No harm done." Vance nudged the notebook away from Steve's hand and closed the cover. "Just take some deep breaths, forget solutions, and think deeply about what a successful life – personal and business – looks like a year from now. What do *you* think, Steve? Take your time."

Steve looked at the window, first at what lay beyond it, but then he focused on the channels of rain. In time, he closed his eyes, and Vance could tell he was blocking out his surroundings, a good first step to finding focus beyond the present and envisioning the future.

Vance sat in silence himself, intermittently watching the rain and turning back to see if Steve was ready to share. He had learned a long time ago, from Charlie, of course, that after you ask a question, just be quiet and give the person time to answer. "The other person knows an answer is expected," Charlie had said, "so it's okay to be quiet for as long as necessary."

After a minute or so, when Vance noticed a slight smile on Steve's face, he knew Steve was finding his way to the answer.

Shortly after, Steve opened his eyes, took an additional few moments of silence, and then told Vance, "I think I know where I want to be a year from now."

"Fantastic! Tell me about it."

Steve took a deep breath and slowly began to speak about the future as if it were the present. "I am attending every one of my kids' meets, games, and school events," he said. "I am home every evening eating dinner with my family. And when I'm home, I'm not sequestered in my office or answering work calls. No, now I am 'present' and giving Amy and the kids my full attention." He sat back against the vinyl. "A year from now I will be comfortable answering Amy when she asks, 'How was work today?' because talking about, or even thinking about work doesn't stress me out anymore."

"Good," Vance said. "Go with that. Build on it. Continue."

Steve closed his eyes again, more quickly finding that introspective and hopeful focus. He began speaking even with his eyes still closed. "I've reconnected with Amy, with my family. I no longer feel like I am leading two lives – work and home." He paused, opened his eyes and maintained eye contact with Vance as he continued. "I no longer give work priority over my family. In fact, it is now the other way around – family first. That's my mantra!" He paused, as if shifting gears; and his prognostication turned to his work life. He spoke of improving his relationships at work, spoke of working hard to reestablish the connection he once had with his team. He spoke of how he had always tried to shield his employees from the problems, too, but that a year from now he would be able to reconnect, to listen and learn about their families, and to care about their lives and how they felt. "We will be a real team again," Steve said. "Kind of like it was in the old days, maybe five years ago, but better because we are moving forward together, not looking back!"

Vance was beaming. "Anything else?" he asked, knowing that sometimes a person gains momentum and comes up with more. He wanted Steve to get it all out, a running stream of consciousness, processing the concept of success from any angle he wanted to.

Steve hesitated, and then said, "I think that's about it. Was that better? Did I give you the kind of answer you were looking for?"

Vance assured him that his response was perfect. He was pleased that Steve had been able to focus on how this year-from-now life would look and how it would make him feel. Client after client, Vance always loved this part the most, because it is often the first time a business owner realizes they are allowed to hope again and that their future can be different than their past or present. When it came right down to it, Vance knew that he was in the business of turning hopelessness into hope realized!

Steve noticed that Vance was smiling and asked him why.

Vance said, "I am smiling because I can help you get to that place of success you have just envisioned. I can help you make all that come true."

"How?"

Vance leaned forward. "Let's take one more step today and we will talk more next week about how it can happen. Are you up for that?"

Steve said, "Are you kidding me? If you can help make all that happen, I will definitely be here. Just tell me what I need to do!"

Vance squinted slightly. "I want you to tell me how much annual revenue you would need to generate to be happy – not simply to get you to a place where you are no longer frustrated, but truly happy."

Steve hesitated, but not long. "Well, I guess I never really thought about it in those terms," he said," but we did $12.3M last year and we lost $120K. I think we were down probably 20% last year and I figure we had dropped roughly that amount every year for the last three years. I guess $16M would make me happy again."

Vance asked, "Why $16M? Why is that the right number?"

"Because I would be profitable again," Steve replied instantly. "I wouldn't be losing any big customers and we would have brought on some new customers, maybe even growing some existing accounts."

"Good," Vance said. "Now then, what big issues would need to be resolved in order for your company to get to $16M in a year?"

Steve thought for a moment, and Vance could tell he was pulling himself back from the kind of thinking that had failed him before. Finally, he said, "I couldn't be involved in every transaction anymore. I would need to rely on others to do work on their own and as a team, apart from me. I would need someone to help me sell, or better yet, someone to take the responsibility for most, or all, of the current client base and new clients. I would need to feel more comfortable that the financial future was going to be better, and not live day-by-day, juggling debt, chasing payments and putting out fires. I would need our company – our *whole* company – working as a team again."

Vance was pleased that Steve was starting to focus on what needed to improve and no longer chasing exact solutions too soon. He loved seeing this transformation, and especially loved seeing it happen so quickly, for it wasn't always that way. He had learned that, unfortunately, most business owners seemed to need to hit rock bottom before they were vulnerable enough to make real changes. Transformational and lasting changes. Steve was a quick study in that regard.

"Steve, we've been here a little over an hour, and made great progress, I think. I've found that sessions like this are most productive when they run from 60 to 90 minutes."

"Okay," Steve said. "What's next?"

Vance said, "I want you to work on these four questions for next week, and to come prepared with details. Give yourself enough time during the week to 'work *on* your business and not in your business.' Here are your four questions, and feel free to write them down and come back to your notes as you need to... First question: How much of your $12.3M will you likely retain this year?" He paused until Steve finished writing. "Second question: What is the average sale amount for a small, medium and large customer?" Another pause. "Third question: How do you want your $16M divided by product?" Steve finished writing and looked up. "And finally," Vance said, "this one: What is the length of your sales cycle for each new client? In other words, how long will it take you to acquire that new client from the first time your company has contacted them?"

Steve looked concerned as he jotted down the last of the questions in his notebook, but then his expression softened. "I can come up with those answers," he said. "I will be ready next week."

"I'm sure you will," Vance reassured him. "We're already zeroing in on where you are and where you want to be. Now we need to map the journey so you can move forward with confidence."

Vance asked for Steve's email address and promised to send a document later that would help him answer the questions and populate the necessary data.

Steve smiled and reached out to shake Vance's hand. He looked then at the Formica tabletop. "Like a cat," he said, picking up the bill for breakfast that Libby had dropped there unnoticed. "This one's on me," Steve said. "And I have a feeling I'll owe you many more!"

CHAPTER EIGHT

No More Important Work Than This

For Steve, the week between meetings at The Fork was rough but hopeful. He and Vance exchanged emails a few times, with Vance providing the promised document to make it easier – although by no means easy – to answer the critical questions meant to be the linchpin for changes that would rescue his business:

1. *How much of your prior year's $12.3M will you likely retain this year?*

2. *What is the average sale amount for a typical small, medium and large customer?*

3. *How should the $16M target revenue be divided by product?*

4. *What is the length of your sales cycle for each new client?*

Steve decided to start with the last question first. But, because the company, or *Steve* to be exact, purchased the CRM but didn't implement it, he had to rely on a series of notes and guesstimates. If only he had just gone ahead and set up that CRM, this question would be easy; but at the time, it simply seemed to be too time-consuming to customize the CRM, upload key data, and then train his team. And since he was often performing a sales role, he didn't really want to fill out that information, let alone ask his sales team to take on what he could already anticipate that they would also see as a time-consuming hassle.

As usual, *time-consuming* was a big problem for Steve. Because normal, everyday business operations took so much of his time and effort, it left little – actually, *no* – time for Steve to tackle the homework Vance had assigned. Still, Steve knew it was necessary work and that Vance was offering a lifeline. So, after a few days of business-as-usual, and with the clock ticking, he moved some appointments, found himself delegating – actually delegating! – tasks others could handle, and sequestering himself behind a closed office door despite the "open-door policy" he liked to be known for.

The one thing Steve did not cancel was evening time with his family. He made a concerted effort to do what should come naturally: spend time with Amy and the kids. He even made it to Seth's swim meet and forced himself to turn off his phone while at the competition. Seth, of course, tried to play it cool with his friends and teammates as teenagers do when they distance themselves from their parents. But one fleeting moment of eye contact between father and son meant the world to Steve. Seth was on the starting blocks for the 100-meter freestyle and he turned to look beyond his goggles and into the spectator stands. When their eyes met, Steve gave an almost imperceptible nod and Seth returned it with an equally subtle grin.

The 100-meter free was not ordinarily Seth's best event, but he swam a personal best, scoring the win by a scant 22 one-hundredths of a second. Steve felt a lump in his throat immediately, and he reflexively laughed out loud, perhaps as a way to halt the tears welling in his eyes.

Yes, he had work to do, it occurred to him, but there could be no more important work than this.

Back at the office the following day, Steve finished his work determining the length of a sales cycle for each new client. He looked at their billing records trying to determine the date each client was converted from prospect to client. In doing so, he was reminded how much faster and accurate this exercise would have been had he actually installed the CRM he purchased.

Next, he tackled the easiest of the remaining questions – the optimal mix of targeted revenue by product. He knew it would be best to have the bulk of their annual revenue rest with their newer products like their inventory management software because they would likely have a longer useful life than the older products, were easier to sell, and also commanded a larger margin.

He then turned his attention to the question regarding the average sale amount for a small, medium and large customer. This was a tough one, and he struggled with determining the method for answering this question as well as the criteria for the customer segmentations. After wrestling with it for about an hour, he called in some of his key personnel: Joe, a senior Salesperson; and Lorenzo, his Project Engineer, for some fresh perspective.

To Steve's surprise – delight, really – they worked well as a team. Ultimately, they determined they needed to first define which customers were small, which were medium, and which were large. After some discussion and healthy debate, they agreed on some meaningful criteria and slotted the clients into Vance's matrix template. Further complicating this answer, however, was the fact that "sales" for each client were not always finite. Some were short-term, one-off sales, but in other cases, an initial sale led to more discovery of what the client truly needed and resulted in an expansion of the original solution provided. And many clients were on a subscription basis, paying a monthly or annual amount for use of the software, so that required calculating and prorating.

No easy answers, Steve thought, but he remembered Vance quoting Oprah Winfrey: "Ask the right questions and the answers will always reveal themselves." Oprah had not promised the answers would come easily, only that they would come. And with the help of his team, come they did.

Finally, he addressed the first question Vance had posed: How much of their annual revenue – $12.3M the prior year – would the company likely retain *this* year? Steve asked Sally, his Accounting Manager, to run some reports on the last few years. It had dawned on him that he could look at a sales report, broken down by sales per customer, to determine how many customers carried over to the next year. While Steve could have easily projected a 20% year-over-year drop, as he had come to believe was the recent unfortunate norm, he dug deeper, going back a few years, essentially creating a year-to-year comparison.

When he had crunched the last of the numbers and looked at the bottom line, the previous year's trends were all too clear – and his heart sank. The business seemed in freefall. They were in much deeper trouble than he had allowed himself to believe.

CHAPTER NINE

Shoofly Pie

Steve arrived a bit early at The Fork and discovered that Vance's corner booth had been taped off, with one of the seats removed. "Darn vinyl finally gave out on that one," Libby said. "Out for repair till next week."

Steve was momentarily "discombobulated," to use an old phrase his mother had often employed. Unsure if Vance had a backup favorite booth, Steve sidled up to the counter and planted himself on a stool near the middle, directly in line with the kitchen.

"Glad to see you back, Honey. You're becoming a regular!" Libby said, smiling broadly as she set a cup of black coffee in front of him. "I'm sure you-know-who will be here shortly. He's pretty much always on time. It's downright annoying at times," she chuckled.

As he waited, his notes on the stool to his left, Steve studied the menu and decided on what he would order when Vance arrived. Then he looked around, taking in the diner from this new vantage point. In the kitchen, he could see a set of eyes and a smidgen (another of his mother's words) of a forehead beneath the white cook's cap of "Bobthecook." (Whenever Vance or Libby or anyone else in the diner mentioned Bob, it was always just that way: *Bobthecook*, as if it were one blended name.)

Bobthecook tapped the bell on the counter and Libby swooped in and gathered up the prepared plates for delivery at the far end of the diner, near Jukebox Jack and his musical machine.

A couple places down from where Steve sat, sharing countertop real estate with condiments and napkin holders, stood a standup sign which read, "Satisfy Your Pie Hunger with a Piece of Wholesome Goodness!" Beneath that declaration, it listed the regular pie flavors available at The Fork: Apple, Cherry, Banana Cream, and Gooseberry. Libby strolled by then, stopped at the sign and placed a "Flavor of the Day" dry-erase sticker on the sign on which she had written "Shoofly Pie!"

"Now what in the world is Shoofly Pie?" Steve asked, stopping Libby in her tracks as she started to dash off.

"Oh, Sweetie, if you haven't tried Shoofly Pie, you haven't lived much now have you?" She leaned in, as if sharing a deeply-held secret family recipe. "Shoofly is a molasses pie, so you can imagine how sweet it is, but it's really kind of like a molasses crumb cake inside a pie crust. We serve it as a wet-bottom Shoofly which comes out like part cake, part pie with a firm but sorta gooey filling." She stood up again and looked past Steve's shoulder. He heard the cowbell on the door signal that someone had just walked in. Libby whispered, "It's great with coffee and it's Vance's favorite," she said, and then yelled toward the end of the diner to Jukebox Jack, "Cue the Shoo, Jack!"

As the jukebox spun to life, with Dinah Shore crooning the 1940s standard, *Shoo-fly Pie and Apple Pan Dowdy*, Steve turned toward the door.

There Vance stood, smiling, eyes closed, and inhaling the rising scent of molasses. "That song and that smell can mean only one thing," he proclaimed. "I've died and gone to heaven!"

Steve leaned closer to Libby and whispered, "A piece for both of us before we leave, on me."

The two men sat at the counter, an empty stool between them to save room for notebooks and papers as necessary. They ordered – Steve choosing a lighter breakfast than originally planned in anticipation of the Shoofly to come.

"Probably a good thing we've been banned from the usual booth," Vance said. Sometimes a change of scenery helps you see things more clearly." He rotated on the stool. "I usually like to face the rest of the restaurant to see all that is taking place, but it *is* easier to see the heart of the operation from here, isn't it?"

Steve nodded and surveyed the counter, the prep area beneath the kitchen window opening, and what he could see in that backroom space. Everything seemed where it needed to be for the diner and its staff to operate efficiently. For the first time, Steve detected a rhythm in the controlled chaos. Even though Libby and Jenny, the young back room server, seemed to be in a near-constant state of hustle, Steve noticed that there was little unnecessary effort, virtually no wasted steps. It was a ballet of sorts, he thought, if you looked deep enough.

"A well-oiled machine," Steve observed.

"Absolutely," Vance agreed, "and that makes having a successful enterprise a little easier, don't you think?"

After a brief recap of their weeks, the food came quickly and the two men ate, making small talk for a while before Vance got down to business. "So, Steve, tell me, how difficult was it to gather the information necessary to answer the questions I posed to you?"

"Well, it certainly makes sense to start with those questions and answers," he said. "Frankly, I thought I pretty much knew the answers to those questions, but when I decided to confirm my assumptions, I realized I didn't know as much as I thought I did about my own company. I had to do some deep thought and research that I hadn't anticipated."

"Any other surprises?"

"Well, yes," Steve confessed. "It was a bit humbling to realize I didn't know how much repeatable business we have each year. I thought we were closer to 80%, but I found out we are only at 72%. For the last three years we have lost an average of 28% of our current revenue. No wonder we have been struggling!"

Vance was nodding slowly and jotting down some figures on a sheet of paper. "Steve, you aren't alone in such a realization. Many companies can't see what's right in front of them. So, with revenue of $12.3M last year, you are likely to retain 72% of your revenue or a bit more than $8.8M. Well, that leaves you with $7.2M in *new* revenue to find beyond your retainable $8.8M if you want to achieve your $16M goal. How does that feel to you?"

Steve shook his head. "It feels discouraging. Actually, a bit scary. I don't know how it will be possible to achieve that goal."

Vance slid his coffee cup forward for Libby to refill the next time by. "Steve, it would be scary if you continued to operate the way you are today, but I am going to help you build a new model where achieving your target revenue is not only possible, it is very likely!"

Steve chuckled and took a deep breath. "Okay, that sounds great to me. I can't see it yet," he said, "but you're the expert! So, what's next?"

Libby swooped in and refilled both their cups. She winked at Vance and rushed off again. He smiled and continued. "We need to build some foundational elements first. The first foundational piece is a 2-year sales forecast. But let's examine the other three questions I posed to you, along with the answers you gathered. What about the question of your average sale by client size? What did you come up with?"

"I struggled with the answers to this question," Steve admitted, "so I decided to gather some of my key personnel together and ask them for help. We looked back at our last five years' sales history, by customer, and realized there are some distinct and natural breakpoints in customer size. Once we determined where those breakpoints occurred, we analyzed the average number of software users at each company."

Vance said, "That all makes a great deal of sense, and I imagine you've never really looked at it in that way or in that detail. How did you enjoy attacking the problem with some of your team members?"

"It felt great," Steve said. "And it was the first time we had joined forces to solve a problem in a long time. So long, in fact, that it wasn't even my initial inclination to approach it that way and include them. But I was glad I invited them to give me a hand on that question. They responded well and seemed to enjoy being part of the solution."

"I'm glad you took that approach," Vance concurred. "While some of the questions and analysis will need to come from you alone, it's good to involve your team when you can. So, what did you come up with?"

Steve ran his finger down his summary page of notes. "A corporate purchase typically ranges from $50,000 through $250,000," he said, "but we discovered the average is $130,000, due to the number of smaller deals we close."

"Great, and that leads us to this key question: How long would it take one of your sales reps to close one of these opportunities?"

Steve exhaled heavily. "Well, it is typically more difficult to close the larger deals, but we believe – at least anecdotally – that it would take six weeks to—"

"Wow, that's pretty quick!" Vance interjected.

Steve raised his right his hand in a "just hold on a minute" gesture. "Unfortunately, our recordkeeping isn't exact, so we don't have a way to go back and figure it out precisely."

Vance smiled and nodded. "Understood. So, are most of your closed deals the result of an existing relationship, a referral, a direct outreach, or some other means?"

"Typically, a strong referral.

"Okay, the speed-to-closing rate makes sense, then," Vance said. "So, if you were reaching out to a new prospect, the length of time to acquire a client would likely be longer then, wouldn't it?"

"I suppose so, but we haven't been very successful targeting and landing new customers lately, and I think the truth is that we were so successful in the past with referrals and our current customers growing that we never really had to learn how. I am not sure we know where to start, I suppose."

Vance took a sip of his coffee and paused a moment to gather his thoughts. Finally, he said, "Okay, I'm getting a sense of where things stand. So, let's move on to the last question. How do you want your targeted revenue of $16M divided by product? What would be the best mix for your company moving forward?"

"I struggled with this one too," Steve confessed, "because I had never thought about it that way before – we were just happy to have the revenue. But our inventory management software is the most profitable, so I would like at least half the sales to come from that product. The other half I would like to have split between our business automation software and resource planning software."

Vance extended his arm and shook hands with Steve. "Good work, Steve! I think this is a great start. Tell me, aside from some important facts and figures, what did you learn going through this process?"

Steve lowered his eyes and reflected for a few seconds. "I learned that I don't know my business as well as I should. I also learned that I have the answers to these questions if I look at the right data and involve the right people. Oprah was right," he said, "Ask the right questions and the answers will reveal themselves."

Vance lowered himself from the stool and stood and stretched a bit. "My back is missing that good ol' corner booth right about now," he said. Still standing and facing Steve, he said, "You now have all the information you need to put together an initial sales forecast and you have the foundation for a new compensation plan, too."

"I do?"

"Yes, sir! You know the revenue you want to achieve and how much revenue will likely repeat from last year. The difference is how much new revenue you need to acquire. You also know, on average, how long it will take to acquire new clients and how much an average sale will be."

"I didn't realize it was so easy."

Vance mirrored Steve's not-so-fast gesture from before. "Of course, there are some additional details needed to fine tune your forecast and build an appropriate compensation plan, but we have a good foundation to build on for next week."

"That's great!" Steve said. His smile was one of optimistic relief.

Vance reached into a folder he had placed on the counter and handed Steve a couple sheets of paper. "I need you to apply what we talked about today with this forecasting template. Here are the instructions, too, but I can email you all this, so you have an electronic copy as well."

Steve skimmed the papers and nodded his head. "I can do this, certainly."

"After you complete these documents, you will have the exact amount of revenue needed by product and by month for the next two years. No longer will you have to wonder what it takes to get to your goals. In other words, you will have built the beginning of a tactical plan to achieve those goals."

Steve rose from the stool. "I do like the sound of that!"

"Steve, my last question for you today is this: How do you feel about the progress we made this morning based on what you learned this week?"

Without hesitation, Steve replied, "I feel like I have hope for the first time in a long time. I'm beginning to believe my future can be not just different, but better!"

"I'm really glad to hear that," Vance said. "And you're right. It *can* be better, if you continue to follow this process. We have a lot of work left to do, but I have no doubt you can accomplish all your dreams!"

The two men were gathering their papers, folders and notebooks when Libby appeared between them and the front door. "Not so fast, fellas," she said, motioning toward the counter behind them. Two plates of Shoofly Pie sat there, warm and tempting.

CHAPTER TEN

Good Hands

As Vance drove away from The Fork after his first full session with Steve, he felt a mix of emotions. He was happy and encouraged that Steve was taking on the challenge so eagerly and earnestly. He was grateful for the opportunity to step in and make a difference for yet another business owner in dire straits. But he was also a little sad that he couldn't share with Charlie what was going on or how, by helping Steve, he was paying forward what Charlie had once done for him.

The loss of Charlie still stung. It had been just a few weeks now, and in some ways, Vance felt as if he had lost a father – or at least a wise older brother – that he hadn't known about until later in life. It might have been easy for Vance to become bitter about losing Charlie so soon, since he still felt he needed Charlie's counsel from time to time; but Vance's faith told him to focus not on the loss but rather on the gift of knowing Charlie at all. Of having Charlie enter his life at just the right time. Of having Charlie as a role model forever forward.

Certainly, Charlie was a blessing. And Vance was determined to take on that mantle, too. With his paying clients, and with Steve, his *student*, Vance knew he had the power – and thus the obligation – to make a difference in their businesses, which would in turn improve their lives and the lives of their families and employees.

On the highway as he drove toward an afternoon client appointment, Vance's thoughts turned to Nancy, Charlie's widow. He wondered how she was doing. More than that, he wondered if she knew, if she truly *knew*, how much of an influence Charlie had on him and surely on others, too. While many expressed that to her during Charlie's memorial service, she could easily have been in a bit of a fog and not really comprehending the words, let alone the sincerity of the sympathetic testimonials.

Now, in the abiding quiet aftermath, Vance wondered if hearing that kind of testimonial again might bring Nancy an extra measure of peace and healing.

Within miles, he recognized the exit, and turned off the highway.

Steve had lingered a few moments after Vance left The Fork, slowly savoring the final morsels of Shoofly Pie and replaying in his mind the session with Vance. As he reflected, it occurred to him that finding this place, finding this man, finding this *opportunity*, felt very much like a blessing. Though Steve was a man of quiet faith, it dawned on him that he had crafted a life so busy that he seldom took time to notice the little miracles around him every day. Amy was one of those miracles, certainly, as were the kids. That much he knew. But as he gathered up the last crumbs of the Shoofly Pie, he realized he had been blessed with many other God-given gifts along the way, too: his "geek" intellect that proved strong enough to spawn a business that had supported not only his family but those of his employees; his innate kindness with others; his trusting nature, too.

But Steve also knew that each of these gifts could also be his downfall. Being too strong a geek and too tethered to the technical side of his business meant he hadn't devoted the time and energy necessary to become the leader his team needed. He knew his company would not have been created unless his technical mind had seen an opportunity to create software that could help manufacturing companies save money and operate more efficiently, but he also knew he struggled to become a complete business owner, and those deficiencies were now at risk of taking down the very company he had worked so hard to build. Steve had read a recent U.S. Small Business Administration article that stated, "over 50% of small businesses fail in the first year and 95% fail within the first five years." His company had beaten the odds, but at this moment he wasn't touting those statistics, given that he was struggling to get to his next company anniversary.

Being too *kind* meant he had probably put his company in financial peril – even though he had quietly cut his own salary in half two years earlier and was maintaining that level even now. In retrospect, he had probably taken that salary cut rather than address certain deficiencies in his team. He knew he had leadership issues that needed work, but he also knew certain members of his team had performance issues *they* needed to improve. But because Steve didn't like conflict, he avoided having the difficult discussions that should have taken place. He now realized that he didn't do those employees, or any employees for that matter, a favor by allowing them to continue operating at an unacceptable level. His avoidance of conflict, along with his desire to be a kind leader, had led the company to a point where all his employees were now at risk if he couldn't turn this around.

And being too *trusting* meant that he put too much faith in the unlikely possibility that things might turn around on their own, that somehow the ship would right itself without a change in course, and that the crew on his ship were the right crew for current and future conditions. Hope is a wonderful attribute, he supposed, but not when used as a business strategy. He was avoiding his reality and not seeking help. He had buried his head in the sand.

It was hard to imagine where he would be in six months if he hadn't met Vance. He was easily trusting him, too, but perhaps out of necessity, out of a growing desperation, without really knowing much about the man. Although Steve believed he had a good intuition about people in general and tended to be a good judge of character, he felt a sudden rush of doubt. Even if Vance seemed like a great guy, a wise and giving man, what did Steve know about Vance's clients? Was he really making a difference in their businesses and in their lives as he had promised to do for Steve? And another thought overwhelmed him now, too: even if Vance's assistance helped Steve turn around his business, what would be the cost? The two had never discussed Vance's fees or compensation expectations. When they reached a critical point in plans to turn things around, would Vance suddenly demand an exorbitant sum to keep things going?

Maybe I'm not as trusting as I thought, Steve considered.

Libby stopped before him to remove the spotless Shoofly plate, and Steve caught her before she could dart away.

"What can you tell me about Vance?"

41

Vance sat in his idling car in front of Charlie and Nancy's house. Perhaps he should have called first, he thought. But before he could fully process that notion, the front door opened and Nancy stepped out. She retrieved the newspaper from the porch and then looked up and shielded her eyes, her gaze attempting to penetrate the glare on Vance's windshield.

When he opened the car door and stepped out, Vance could see instant relief on Nancy's face. She smiled and waved him toward her.

Libby poured herself a glass of water, stepped from behind the counter and took a seat on the stool to Steve's right.

He swiveled his own stool to face her. "I probably shouldn't ask such a loaded question when you are on the clock," he said.

Libby dismissed the comment with a wave-off gesture of her hand. "Honey, I will use any excuse I can to take a load off my feet for even a few minutes." She sipped her water, exhaled heavily and then pursed her lips in thought. A few seconds later, she addressed Steve's question. "What can I tell you about Vance, huh? Well, I reckon if I had to give you a one-word answer, that word would be 'genuine.' With Vance, what you see is what you get. He is kind and considerate and personable – and sharp as a tack – as you've surely noticed, but also driven. Even in that drive, however, he's genuine and giving. He believes we all have untapped potential – some of us more than others, I suppose – and he is at his happiest when he is helping worthy people *untap* theirs."

Steve nodded but tried to dig a little deeper. "I know he told me a little about his background, but I realized we have been meeting for the last few weeks and I don't really know him..." He hesitated, unsure if he should go on, or if Libby was even the right person to ask. "I'm mostly curious about two things at this point – and purely from a selfish perspective. First, is Vance really good at helping struggling businesses find their way – businesses like mine, I mean? And second, assuming he is genuinely good at what he does and can help untap our potential, what does something like that cost; I mean, he and I haven't discussed what he charges yet, so—"

Libby cut in. "Sweetie, I can tell you that in the time Vance has been doing his sales leadership consulting that, number one, he loves it," she said, raising her fingers as she counted, "number two, he's darn good at it based on the stories I've heard and testimonials I've seen, and number three, for

Vance it's not so much a job these days as it is a, um, a *calling*. Yes, that's the word he used, a calling."

The counter bell rang, Bobthecook interrupting her short break.

"As for what he charges," Libby said, stepping down from the stool, "he doesn't say, and I don't ask. But if you're concerned about that, I'm sure he won't be bothered if you bring it up since he hasn't."

The "pop in" visit with Nancy was lovely but brief. She was leaving soon to visit her daughter and grandson, to babysit for the boy, actually, saying she was grateful for the distraction and for feeling useful. She was grateful, too, that Vance shared how much Charlie meant to him and that he was paying forward Charlie's kindness with someone in need.

"There can be no greater compliment than that," Nancy had said. "I'm just glad Charlie had a sense of that, with clients and friends and family members, before he passed. I know his legacy is in many good hands now." With that, Nancy had taken Vance's hands in hers, and then hugged him and whispered, "Thank you for carrying Charlie in your heart as you help others. I think that keeps his spirit alive, don't you?"

Now, back on the road, Vance's thoughts kept shifting between Nancy and Steve. Before long, a text message came through and Vance pushed the button on his dashboard screen to hear an audible version of the message: *"Thank you for working with me. I am excited to see where this leads. One question. What will I owe you as we move forward and when will you expect payment? Steve."*

Vance smiled and thought for a moment before pushing the microphone icon on the screen and dictating his hands-free response: *"You are welcome. My pleasure. Excited about the possibilities myself. Don't worry too much about the bill. You will be pleasantly surprised. I will bring an initial invoice next week."* He pushed a button to send the message and laughed out loud, an idea for the so-called "invoice" already forming in his head.

CHAPTER ELEVEN

For the Good of the Cause

When Steve entered The Fork, ready for his next session, Libby was in the newly reupholstered corner booth across from Vance and an Elvis tune was playing on the jukebox. The song was an unfamiliar one and Steve stopped for a moment just inside the door, searching his memory and trying to get a fix on it. Coming up empty, he stepped toward Libby and Vance.

"Good morning, you two." They looked up at Steve and smiled. Libby started to rise. "Don't let me interrupt or chase you off," Steve said.

"No worries at all, dearie," Libby replied. "Probably need to get back at it anyway." Just then, Bobthecook tapped the bell, signaling an order ready for pickup. "See," Libby said, "no rest for the weary."

Before she dashed away, Steve asked, "What is that Elvis song playing on the juke box? I don't recognize that one."

"It's called *'If I Can Dream,'* I think," she said. "Oh, and guess what the pie of the day is?"

"Elvis is your clue," Vance interjected.

Steve pursed his lips for a moment. "Ummm, well, I'm guessing it's not a King Cake since that's not a pie…"

"Nope," Libby beamed, "it's Peanut Butter 'n 'Nana Pie. Delicious as always. Plenty to go around if you want some." With that, she disappeared, and Steve took his place across from Vance, placing a folder on the seat beside him.

"How was your week?" Vance asked.

"Good, thanks. What I mean is that there were no new bad surprises, I guess. I feel a bit more hopeful and empowered just knowing the scope of my situation."

"That's an excellent position from which to make changes, don't you think?"

Steve took a deep breath. "I think so. There's just one thing bothering me, and it's been bothering me for a while."

"What's that?" Vance asked.

"It's what I texted you about. The money thing." Steve pulled a napkin from the dispenser and laid it on the table in front of him. He turned it each direction, fidgeting. "Vance, I have every confidence that you can help, and Libby tells me how wonderful you are, too—"

"She may be a bit biased."

Steve continued: "And I am so grateful for what you've already done, but I need to know what your services will cost me. As you know, things are really tight right now…"

Vance raised his hand, gesturing for Steve to wait a moment. Then, he reached into a case on the seat beside him and produced two candy bars. He placed them on the table in front of Steve, a *Zero* bar and a *100 Grand* bar. "Which do you prefer, Steve?"

Steve looked at Vance, obviously confused. "I have a feeling there's a right answer and a wrong answer here."

Vance laughed. "You are not letting me get by with any theatrics, are you?" He pushed forward the 100 Grand bar. "My services could be worth this much or more to your organization; certainly, the impact on your bottom line will be much greater than 100 grand." Next, he pushed forward the Zero bar. "But this, Steve, is my invoice. You'll owe me nothing."

"But—"

Vance continued: "That is, you'll owe me nothing IF you take this seriously and do what's required to turn your business around. I know you are capable of making the necessary changes and hard decisions, so your determination and your eventual success will be my reward."

Steve shook his head, incredulous. "Vance, that's so generous, but I, I just, well, I just don't get it. Of course, I'll do what needs to be done. But... I mean, how can you do this? How can you afford to do this? Surely, you don't do this for all your clients."

"You're right, Steve. I don't do this for all my clients. In fact, you're the first one. It's kind of like an attorney taking a case *pro bono*, for the good of the cause."

"But why me? I mean, don't all your clients have a similar critical need?"

Vance held up his coffee cup when he caught Libby's eye. "Right with ya," she called out.

"My clients come to me in varying stages of distress, you could say. Some desperate, others less so, but all are at some stage of trouble – pain, you could say. And if it makes you feel any better, I'll be spending less time with you than I typically spend with a client. Normally, I immerse myself more fully into their operations, spending one or two days a week with them, some of that time on-site, even. With you, I have full confidence that you can implement the execution of what we discuss here."

Libby sidled up to the table, filled Steve's coffee mug and refilled Vance's. "Be right back for your orders."

Vance took a cautious sip of the steaming brew. "Steve, do you remember me mentioning Charlie, my old mentor, who passed away recently?"

"Yes, I remember you talking about him."

"The truth is I owe a debt to Charlie that I can never repay to him directly. So, I just have this unshakeable feeling of needing to honor his legacy. I have felt it since the first time I overheard you talking about your situation. Charlie's voice inside my head keeps nudging me to pay it forward. That's where you come in."

"That's certainly generous and kind and...," Steve began. "But again, why me?"

"Why not you? After all, right place, right time, right opportunity, yes? In any event, this is where we are. This is my offer, and this is my invoice. You will owe me zero. Okay with you?"

Steve was shaking his head, trying to find the words. "I am humbled, of course. And so very grateful. But I can't accept charity, Vance."

Vance started to speak, but Steve stopped him. "I know, you are repaying a debt and I'm the benefactor. Very well, I accept. But at the very least, Vance, I will buy you breakfast, lunch, whatever you want from The Fork, for as long as you want it. Beyond that, all I can offer is eternal gratitude – and the commitment to do the hard work necessary."

Vance looked down, his face suddenly flushed. He extended his hand to Steve and they shook in agreement. "Then let's get down to business," Vance said.

"Did you bring your new sales forecast with you?" Vance asked. He then took a syrupy bite of the "hubcap" pancake Libby had just delivered.

"Sure did," Steve replied. He pulled a paper from the folder beside him.

"How did the process go?"

"It went well, I think. By answering your questions, I had the info I needed to fill out the form. Your directions helped a lot, too."

Vance avoided looking at the figures on the paper in Steve's hand. "What did you learn while going through that process?"

Steve hurriedly chewed a bite of thick-cut bacon, then said, "I learned that I never considered the timing of *when* revenue was likely to come in. I had never been concerned about that before; the money just came in when it came in. But now, with sales down so much, my lack of insight into future revenue does matter. And because I hadn't set any expectations, I couldn't hold myself or my team accountable. Because of that, I only know if we are behind or ahead after it's already too late."

Vance nodded, a look of familiar understanding on his face.

"I also hadn't considered the different sizes of deals or the length of the sales cycle," Steve continued. "Looking back, it's obvious to me now that we were constantly in reaction mode. We never planned ahead for what we wanted to happen, let alone *when* we wanted it to happen."

"Very good," Vance said. "Think of this forecast as your itinerary. It tells you where you are going and when you want to get there. No longer will you take this trip not knowing where you are going or the route to get there."

Steve nodded in agreement. "Yep, I guess that's what we were doing."

Vance pushed his half-empty coffee cup toward the edge of the table, a sign to Libby that the need for a refill was imminent when she had a moment.

"It's also important," he said, to remember that your forecast isn't a static document; it is meant to change as needed. Once you gain information that causes you to change your path, do so. You wouldn't want to set off on your trip, find out that the road you are on won't get you where you want to go, but not change direction, would you?"

"No, definitely not."

"Well, this is much the same. Track your progress against your goals and change direction as necessary. Big changes or small. Major corrections or minor ones."

"Got it," Steve agreed.

"Now let's discuss compensation plans. Tell me how you pay your sales reps today."

Steve took a sip of coffee and followed Vance's lead, pushing his cup toward the edge of the table. "We pay a 3% commission on all sales."

"On all sales," Vance repeated. "So, they receive 3% commission, regardless of product sold?"

"Yes, that's correct."

"But you mentioned last week that each product was not equally profitable."

"Correct."

Vance shifted in his seat. "And yet you pay the same commission amount for each product. You see where I'm headed here, right?"

"I never thought of it that way," Steve said. "Yes, we have the best margin on our inventory management software."

"Okay, let me ask another question… Do you value the revenue from a new customer the same way you value revenue from an existing customer?"

"Well, I appreciate all revenue, especially on equally profitable products, but it is a lot harder to find new customers than to keep existing customers. Frankly, Vance, we haven't done very well attracting new customers for a while."

"Why do you think that is?"

Steve grinned. "I imagine you are going to tell me it has something to do with their compensation plan."

"Again, you are on to me. Yes, it is definitely connected to your sales comp plan. The bottom line is this, Steve: You want to develop a compensation plan that incents the kind of behavior you are seeking – the exact amount of revenue, by product, by month, by rep. You want a compensation plan that allows your reps to win when you do and lose when you do; that way you're all motivated to achieve the same results – the *best* results."

Libby stopped by and topped off the cups. "Anything else at the moment, fellas?"

"Nothing yet," they said in unison.

Libby looked at them suspiciously. She whispered to Steve, "You're startin' to sound like this one," she said, nodding toward Vance. "Just sayin'...."

Vance smiled, shaking his head, and then continued to lead the discussion. "Okay, so last week we determined your ideal revenue, by product, because you needed to figure out what you wanted to happen first. On top of that, the document I gave you asked you to place that revenue in the months you would like to have that revenue come in. You can't create an incentive program to do particular things, until you first determine what you want to occur and when."

Steve nodded.

Vance took a couple bites of the pancake and washed it down with the coffee. "So, the ideal compensation plan motivates your reps to take the actions that help them make the most amount of money. If you've written the plan correctly, they will be motivated to do exactly what you want. They will make money when you do! No longer will you have to tell them what you want them to do, they'll want to take those actions because it benefits them."

"That makes perfect sense."

"Okay," Vance continued, "so, let's go back to what you want. What do you want your reps to sell the most of and when do you want them to sell it?"

"Well," Steve began, "as we discussed, I want them to sell more inventory management software than our business automation and resource planning software."

"How much more?"

"I'm not sure."

"Actually, you are sure," Vance said. "How did you break your $16m revenue target down between those three products?"

"Oh, right. I did already figure that out."

"Yes, you sure did. And because you've done that, you will want to set targets for your reps proportional to what you set for your company."

"Got it," Steve said.

"Now, what else do you want? What else does your company need in order to hit your targets?"

"Well, let me think," Steve said, taking a moment before responding. Finally, he said, "I need new customers, of course."

"How much in revenue from those new customers?"

"Wait, I already know this – $7.2 million!"

"Exactly! And I believe you told me it's harder to acquire a new customer than keep an existing customer, correct?"

"Yes, that's correct."

Vance pushed on. "Then you want to pay a higher commission for new customers than retaining existing customers, right?"

"Just because it's harder?" Steve questioned. "If my customers are equally valuable based on the same products, why does it matter if they are new or not? I don't want my reps to ignore my existing customers or I will lose more than the 28% I'm already losing."

"You are right. That's why the key is how you proportionally pay for new and existing customer sales. You want to motivate your reps to acquire new customers, while having them recognize that they still make good money holding onto existing customers. You can also incent them to grow existing sales, thus reducing your 28% client retention rate."

"That would be great," Steve said. "I want it all, I guess!" He chuckled. "Whatever gets me to my $16M goal faster!"

"There are many different strategies that can be employed to build the proper compensation plan and incent what you would like to take place, Steve. Bonuses, SPIFF's, draws, commission – each motivates a different type of behavior."

"I didn't realize there were so many different types."

"There sure are," Vance said. Okay, lastly, let's talk about how you should balance salary with variable compensation."

"Okay."

"I know you didn't have quotas for your reps previously, but if they did what you expected them to do, how much would they have made?"

"I would say about $80,000 a year."

"And how much of that $80,000 would be salary and how much would be commission?"

"Their salaries are slightly different, but on average, about $60,000 would be in the salary portion."

"And how much commission do they make now on an average year?" Vance asked.

"About $12,000."

"And that $12,000 is earned currently on existing customers?"

"Yes."

"So, in essence," Vance said, "there is only $8,000 in additional commission payouts per sales rep they are missing out on?"

"Yes, that's correct."

"Could they live comfortably on $72,000?"

"I think so."

Vance leaned back. "Steve, therein lies your problem. There's an old saying that you want your sales reps 'to be able to eat hamburger, but not steak' on their salary."

"I've never heard that before."

It basically means that your reps are eating steak already, so there isn't much more motivation to work really hard to make the extra $8,000. They make $60,000 in salary and another $12,000 in commission and they haven't produced a single new customer."

Steve shook his head. "Wow, I never thought of it that way!"

"Your sales reps have been winning even though your company has been losing revenue. You have not been equally yoked."

"I can see that now, Vance. Thank you for making that clear."

"There's more," Vance said. "In addition, your compensation plans should change each year."

"Why is that?"

"Because your goals change, what you want to happen changes, and your sales team needs to be compensated for what you currently want to happen, not what you wanted years before."

"I get it," Steve said. "I have never changed our plan, but now I see why that has hurt me."

"You're a good student," Steve. "That makes things so much easier. Now, for next week, I want you to consider the compensation plan components we talked about and then we can look at what you put together."

"Sounds good!"

Vance pushed away the last remnants of the hubcap pancake and picked up his white napkin and waved it. "I surrender," he said.

"What, no Peanut Butter 'n 'Nana pie?" Steve asked? "Remember, it's all my treat from here on out!" And at that, Vance turned up his collar, curled his lip and said, in his best Elvis voice, "Thank you. Thank you very much!"

CHAPTER TWELVE

A Special Kind of Secret Magic

The drive back to the office was a time of reflection for Steve. Vance's offer to help save his company *pro bono* was humbling, to say the least. Beyond that, it was also surprising, perhaps even shocking. Steve was so often caught up in the daily difficulties of running his business that he had forgotten to look for opportunities to serve other people. He had been so inwardly focused, trying so hard to turn around his flailing business that he had ignored his wife, children, employees, and just about everyone around him. Yes, he was still present in their lives, but he was "taking" a lot more than he was "giving." The worst part is that he didn't realize the metamorphosis that had taken place. Steve had always prided himself on being a person that found joy in giving more than taking, but somehow that had changed, and he didn't like the person he had become. Vance's selfless act had jolted him and caused him to take stock of who he was, and more importantly, who he wanted to get back to being. Steve pledged to himself that he was going to look for opportunities to return to the servant-focused person he was before his company took a bad turn. He hoped he could perform a similar kindness for someone else one day.

Turns out that day was *this* day for a small act of kindness.

When Steve stopped at a fast food restaurant drive-thru window to grab a soft drink, he looked in his mirror at the car behind him. It was an older model car that had seen better days and now looked destined for the scrap heap. It belched smoke and when Steve lowered his car window, he could hear the car's engine sputtering.

Inside the noisy and rickety machine was a young woman, perhaps in her mid-twenties. She looked a bit disheveled and was clearly trying to control the three children Steve could see in the car with her. In that moment, Steve felt a flash of guilt and embarrassment. Who was he to ever feel sorry for himself? Sure, things were tough at work and needed turned around as soon as possible; but when he watched that young mother in the mirror, he felt very fortunate indeed. After all, he was driving a nice car, made a good living, had a great family and a beautiful home. He had money in his pocket and would have money there tomorrow as well. Could the woman in the car say the same? He felt a beckoning he hadn't felt for a long time. His mind instantly drifted back to a sermon delivered by his pastor many years ago that challenged the congregation to have "people eyes." People eyes were described as a proactive effort to look for opportunities to connect and help people. To not only take advantage of opportunities that were obvious to all, but to *intentionally* seek out the more obscure opportunities to connect and help people. Steve instantly knew that this was a small opportunity to make a difference in someone's life, in the same way that Vance had obviously done for him. And although his act wouldn't be to the level of Vance's kindness and grace, it was a start.

Steve pulled up to the drive-thru window. He opened his wallet and handed the cashier a $50 bill. "This should take care of my order and the one for the car behind me," he said. "With whatever is left, I'll leave it up to you to pass it on to someone else in need or keep it yourself if that person is you."

The cashier's jaw dropped. Speechless, she handed Steve his drink, and he drove away without looking back.

Vance had a somewhat light workday after leaving the diner. He took care of some emails and prepared a worksheet he would review on-site with a client the next day. It was a beautiful day outside, sunny and warm – *Chamber of Commerce weather*, he'd heard it called. So, Vance drove to the park near his home. He got out of his car and sat at a picnic table watching couples walk their dogs and children kick balls into nets on soccer fields.

He noticed the chubby bellies on fledgling birds and the red tuft on the head of a Woodpecker. He noticed the wind twisting a dozen remnant leaves into an invisible vortex a few feet away. He noticed wildflowers greeting the sun's warmth on the fringe of walking trails. And sticks laying on the ground, ready to be picked up by a child who could pretend it into a magic wand and then have that wand work a special kind of secret magic only *that* child could conjure.

Magic.

It occurred to Vance that there was plenty of magic around if you thought to look for it. Even more if you dared to make it yourself. This was something Charlie had taught him – how to look for opportunities to make a difference in the lives of other people. Magic or not, it seemed like wizardry to the person receiving the gift, but it was really just good old-fashioned kindness. His chance meeting with Steve had really brought back vivid memories of Charlie and all that he had taught him. It was difficult to think of Charlie, given his recent passing, but it also made him smile to think about his wonderful friend and mentor. Lately, he couldn't tell if the welling tears were from sadness or joy; perhaps they were both. Vance thought Charlie would have been proud of him today, proud of his focus on serving and not on money.

He walked back to his car and reached in, retrieving the 100 Grand bar Steve had left with him after accepting the Zero bar as Vance's quote for services. Since Vance had declined the Peanut Butter 'n 'Nana Pie this time, he sated his mild hunger now with the chocolate bar.

As he took bite after slow bite, Vance thought about the difference between the names of the two candy bars. Not just about the difference between zero and a hundred grand, but rather about the difference between having a little and having a lot, between being desperate and being comfortable. He thought back one more time to the day's events and again felt good about helping Steve, not so much because Steve had the greatest need of anyone, but because he felt confident that Steve, somewhere, someday, would use the learning experience for an even greater good.

Vance smiled at the thought, finished his snack, threw the candy bar wrapper into a trash can nearby, and then walked back to his car.

In the field on the other side of the parking lot, Vance watched as a young boy kicked a ball into a net. When he ran to retrieve the ball, the boy stopped in his tracks. He knelt and picked up a stick. Studied it. And grinned.

CHAPTER THIRTEEN

On a Mission

It had been a different kind of week for Steve. Even though his work load had not decreased – in fact, he was doing more than ever since he was in the process of gathering and analyzing information for his sessions with Vance in addition to his normal duties – Steve had still managed to make it home for dinner every night with the family. What at first had seemed awkward – with the kids looking at him as if to say, "What are *you* doing here again?" – eventually felt pleasantly *normal*.

There were still moments of silence around the dining room table, of course; Seth, in particular, was in that awkward teenage "I don't feel like talking" phase. But for Steve, it was simply nice to be in the company of his wife and kids in the evening rather than being sequestered in his office drinking coffee and snacking on vending machine potato chips. It occurred to him mid-week that despite the heaping portions at The Fork, he was eating better and *feeling* better these days, too.

When he stepped inside the diner, Libby had just finished marking up the daily pie signboard: *Try, Buy, This American Pie!* "Mornin', Steve," she chirped, and then cupped her hands and said, "Hey, Jack, drive the Chevy to the levee!" And with that, the jukebox coaxed forth the voice of Don McLean: *A long long time ago…*

"Okay, I'll bite," Steve said, "What is the Try, Buy, This American Pie made of?"

Libby stepped over to the pie case and brought forth not a round pie pan, but rather a rectangular one that contained a red, white and blue mélange of American pride. Resting beneath scattered stars cut from pie crust dough were mixed strawberries and blueberries.

"Too pretty to eat," Steve said, "but it does look yummy."

"Just take a picture and then you won't feel guilty about messing it up," Libby suggested.

Steve unholstered his phone and snapped a photo. "Will you have an extra pie for me to take home?" he asked. "The family is clamoring for the latest and greatest."

"Sure thing," Libby said. "Ever since you started coming in, we've been baking an extra pie each week!"

The cowbell over the door clanged and Steve turned as Vance walked in. "Libby bending your ear again?" Vance asked, with a wink.

"Other way around," Steve confessed, and the two men took their places in the customary corner booth.

Vance started. "Ever wonder why I never offer to trade seats with you, Steve?"

"Not really. I know that people get attached to a particular place, that ol' comfort zone thing. I mean, I always sit at the same place at the dining room table."

"Well, it's partly that," Vance said, "but it's also because there can be a lot of visual distractions if you sit where I do. That's great if you're just enjoying a breakfast while 'people watching,' but not so great if you need to focus and listen and learn."

Steve nodded. "I see what you mean. Kind of like at work. Sometimes there are too many distractions to be able to concentrate and get things done. I guess that's why I've stayed late at work so many times, just trying to find some quiet."

"And how has that been working for you?"

"Not that great, frankly. After all the noise of the day, being alone in that big building late at night gets *too* quiet, and it seems like the silence just makes the voices in my head louder and louder, reminding me of all the problems."

"Is it still that way, Steve?"

"Lately, not so much. It's still busy and noisy at the office, of course, but I've found that recently I'm able to tune out the noise and focus better."

"Why do you suppose that is?"

Steve furrowed his brow. "Well, I think it must be because I have a sense of purpose. I have a destination and a deadline and, well, I have a sense of *direction* now. That seems to quiet the voices."

Vance smiled. "I certainly like hearing that," he said.

Steve leaned forward. "You're probably gonna think I'm crazy, Vance, but the other day one of those negative voices crept in and started to fill me with doubt and fear again."

"And did you let that voice take root?"

"No sir. I said, right out loud, 'Shut up! I'm on a mission here!'"

Vance laughed loudly. "Good for you, Steve. That's exactly the right thing to do."

"Of course, Sally, one of my sales reps, popped her head in to check on me," Steve continued. "I just looked at her and said, 'Well, I *am* on a mission, and you might just hear me say that again from time to time!'"

"I'm on a mission, too, gents." It was Libby. "My mission – and yes, I choose to accept it – is to fill your cups and take your orders and fill your bellies."

Bobthecook was faster than normal, so before Vance and Steve could get down to serious business, their breakfasts arrived. They made mostly small talk while eating. Steve again thanked Vance for being so generous and Vance waved off the praise. Vance told Steve about taking some time to enjoy the park; and Steve told Vance about dinners with the family, about swim meets and softball and their plans for a new tradition: family movie night. What Steve didn't tell Vance about was what he had done at the drive-thru on the way home from their meeting last week. Doing something like that, even something that small in scope, gave him a glimmer of insight into the kind of psychological reward Vance would earn from his pro bono consulting.

With dishes cleared and coffee cups cheerfully filled by the ever-attentive Libby, Vance turned the discussion to business.

"So, how did it go last week?"

"Pretty well, I think," Steve said. "I took into consideration all we discussed, and I put together an outline for a compensation plan." He dug into his folder and pulled out two copies of the plan, placing one in front of Vance and keeping one for himself.

Vance pulled a pair of reading glasses from his pocket and studied the plan. "This is good, Steve. Looks like you've taken our discussion to heart and turned it into an actionable plan. I think you are ready to put this into its final form."

"Great!"

"Now," Vance continued, "in addition to putting the compensation plan into a digestible format for yourself and everyone affected by it, you'll need to provide each sales rep with a spreadsheet detailing the numeric breakdown of the plan, along with a written plan that describes how the plan will be executed. The written plan will need to be signed by each salesperson."

"Really? Why is that?" Steve wondered. "I've never done that."

"Because signing the written compensation plan is your reps' way of telling you they understand the plan, that they understand its components, its details. Without a signature, a future conversation can be very different and even difficult or at the very least uncomfortable."

"How so?"

Vance shifted in his seat, moving his eyes out of the sudden glare from the sun coming in the window as it cleared a grove of trees outside. "Imagine Harry – that's one of your salespeople as I recall – imagine Harry coming to you in the middle of the year and he says, 'I didn't know that's how my compensation is calculated.' You would enter into a discussion where you would be debating *how* the compensation plan is constructed and reiterating what you originally told him when you first delivered the new plan. Now, imagine that Harry had signed the plan. You could say, 'Now, Harry, you signed the plan committing to your understanding of the plan.' Harry's response would be something like, 'Well, I must have forgot.'"

"Yes, I guess that *would* make a difference."

"Yes, it would," said Vance. "Now, here are some templates you can work on," he said, riffling through a folder on the seat beside him. "Just fill these out and you'll be ready to sit down with each member of your sales team and review their new compensation plans."

"Ok, will do."

"One more thing," Vance continued. "After you deliver the new plan, ask each sales rep this question: 'Now, based on this new compensation plan, what activities will you undertake to maximize your income?' If they give you the right answer, you are in business. If they don't, go back and spend more time with them so they understand what activities you are incenting them to undertake, and the result will be a win-win for both of you."

Steve shook his head in agreement. "That makes sense. Otherwise I would trust that they understand what to do when we might not be on the same page at all."

"That's exactly right. Now, let's shift our attention to your sales personnel. Tell me a bit about each person."

Before Steve could start, Libby stopped by again. "Going to take a short break, fellas; you need anything in the next few minutes?"

"Nothing else for me," Vance said.

Steve added, "Just the check after a bit – it can wait; and when you get a chance, box up that American Pie before I go. I'll buy it even before I try it."

"You won't regret it, Sweetie!"

After Libby left, Steve said, "She's the best, isn't she?"

"One of a kind, that woman," Vance said. Steve detected a tone of genuine affection in Vance's voice; he wondered how far back Vance and Libby went.

"You were about to tell me about your sales team," Vance prodded.

"Yes, okay, first is Joe," Steve said. He handed Vance a sheet of paper. "I prepared bio sheets for each of our salespeople in case you need it as we discuss them. Now, as you'll see here, Joe is probably close to 50 years old, and has been in sales his whole life, mainly in business development. He is primarily focused on retaining and growing our current customers, in addition to bringing on new customers. He has been in software his whole life. In fact, I hired him mostly because of his experience in software. He told me he was sure he could bring over some of his existing customers. He is dependable enough, but not really exceptional in his role."

"Did he bring over any of his previous customers?"

"No," Steve admitted. "He said they wouldn't leave his old company. He said they missed him but didn't want to start over with a new product and company."

Vance nodded and made a note in his notebook. "That's typically the case, Steve, despite a sales rep believing the contrary. I know you didn't assign quotas, but does he meet or exceed your expectations on a regular basis? Before you answer that, consider overall sales generated, new clients attained, existing clients retained, and product mix of the sales generated."

"No, not really," Steve said slowly. "But he has been with me for a long time and everyone really loves Joe."

"I see." Another note. "Tell me about your next salesperson."

"Okay, next we have Sally," Steve said, pushing her bio sheet across the table toward Vance. "She's in her mid-twenties, and this is her second job out of college. Her first job was in inside sales, but she wanted to move to outside sales, and I believed she was capable of it. She's in business development for us. Truth is, she hasn't driven much revenue yet, but she is still very raw. I haven't had much time to work with her, but she is eager, energetic and personable. I feel badly that I haven't spent more time with her, but I have just been so busy."

"Ok, now tell me about your other salesperson," Vance said without looking up, still jotting down his thoughts.

"Finally, we have Harry," said Steve, handing the last bio sheet to Vance. "Now Harry is the most talented of our three salespeople. Late 30's, and he has worked in three different software companies, all in business development roles. Harry is more adept at closing new business, but he's also more of a loner. A bit of a renegade, too, so he doesn't always follow the desired practices."

Vance stopped writing and looked Steve in the eye. "Tell me, what do you do when Harry doesn't follow your desired practices?"

Steve looked away. He cleared his throat. "Well, um, he's my top salesperson, so I honestly don't do too much. I mean, what can I do, really? With sales declining as much as they have, I don't want to upset him and have him leave."

"And how do Joe and Sally react to Harry being able to play by a different set of rules?"

"I don't know for sure," Steve admitted. "But they do occasionally make off-handed comments, so I don't think they like it."

"Okay, so tell me, Steve, if you had to rank Joe, Sally and Harry based on their ability to reach their goals, how would you rank them? Consider not only their ability to reach the goals you've set for them, but really focus on what you want from them in the future, not what they have already accomplished. Also, consider their willingness to change to this new model, including your focus on new customers, how you want half the sales from inventory management software, etc. With that in mind, who are the people that can get you to where you want to go, not where you have already been?"

"Wow, that's a lot to think about," Steve said.

"I know. And this too: while you're considering your answer, be prepared to discuss your rationale behind your ranking."

"More pressure…"

"If this was easy, Steve, you wouldn't need me, now would you?" Vance said with a wry smile.

Steve stared out the window for a few moments. Finally, he said, "I think I would rank them, from top to bottom, Harry, Joe, and then Sally."

Vance cocked his head slightly. "How much did you consider Harry's willingness to adapt to this new model, his willingness to follow the rules or not follow them, and the impact of his attitude on Joe, Sally and the rest of the company?"

"Well, I really just focused on sales performance."

"I want you to consider the whole picture here, Steve, because it's more about where you *need* them to go, than it is about where they've been."

"Okay, in that case then, I would probably put Joe in front of Harry . . . and I might even put Sally in front of Harry, if I could give her some more training."

"Perfect!" Vance exclaimed. "It's often hard to consider firing your top salesperson, or at the very least, having a hard discussion with your top salesperson and hoping they don't leave. But oftentimes a top salesperson does more damage to the entire team's performance than they do to help it. Even worse, their behavior is often not isolated to inside the company, but is often felt by customers, as well. Our primary goal is to have Harry follow the same rules that Joe and Sally follow. If he can do that, he can stay. If he can't, he will need to go. Many companies realize addition by subtraction when their top salesperson leaves."

"That's tough," Steve said. "I understand the rationale, but if it comes to that, it will sure be hard."

Vance agreed. "Anything worthwhile is often difficult. Now, from your bio sheets, I noticed that all three salespeople have manufacturing software experience. Was that by design or luck?"

"No, that was by design. This can be a difficult sale and I don't think anyone without our product experience can be successful selling here."

"I see," Vance said. He took a deep breath. "Steve, in your estimation, is lack of product knowledge the reason that your sales reps don't sell more?"

Steve paused for a moment. "Well, no, I don't think so. I think they have the product knowledge they need."

"So, what *is* the reason?"

"Umm, well…" Steve struggled for a moment. "I guess I'd have to say…maybe they simply aren't skilled enough salespeople."

"So, it isn't lack of product knowledge, but lack of sales skills?"

"I guess so. I never thought about it like that until now."

Vance leaned in. "Steve, let me share something with you. You've just uncovered a common misconception. Many people believe they need to hire the best salesperson in their industry. Let me repeat that: *in their industry*. But that thought process assumes that you need more product knowledge to be successful, when you already have a whole company with that kind of knowledge. Given that you are struggling finding new customers, shouldn't you find someone that is very gifted at that skill – at *selling*?"

"I suppose so."

"Now, imagine what would happen if a new sales rep, with great business development skills, brought you many new opportunities. Could you, or someone else with great product knowledge, go with them to help them in the one area they are deficient?"

"Sure," Steve agreed. "I wouldn't mind going with them on a viable opportunity. Carl, our Product Engineer, could also go along. He's very good with clients, too, very capable of explaining technical aspects in a non-geeky way."

"So, can you see how that would drive more sales than the alternative of focusing only on using the best salesperson in a particular industry?"

"Yes, that makes sense."

Vance leaned back again. Steve noticed how Vance used his body language – leaning forward to emphasize important points and leaning back to indicate when Steve "got it."

Vance continued: "You want to go 'fishing' in the biggest pond possible, and that 'pond' is all salespeople, not just the ones with a particular product knowledge."

"I never thought of it that way. I guess I was blinded by what I thought was the requirement of product or industry knowledge. In the process, I was inadvertently limiting our potential."

"You aren't alone in that thinking. I am sometimes confronted with that objection, too, when it comes to leading sales teams where I don't have the company's product or industry knowledge. It doesn't make any difference in that arena either."

"Well, at least others are afflicted with the same shorts-sightedness I had!"

"Steve, the key is to determine as quickly as possible whether you have the right people in the right roles – you might say 'whether they are in the right seats on the bus.' Now, by the end of the next 90 days you need to make that determination."

"How will I do that?"

"You'll need to travel with your reps and see them in action in front of their current and prospective customers. You'll need to conduct weekly meetings with each salesperson to gain an understanding of their capabilities, strengths, weaknesses and ability to perform at the expected standards. And you'll need to implement your new compensation plan *now*, so your salespeople are financially rewarded for the sales you desire – and the sales you *need* if you are to turn things around."

"Okay. I'm in," said Steve. "Some surprising stuff today, Vance. Thanks for opening my eyes and putting me on the right path."

Apparently sensing the two men had concluded their deep discussion, Libby stepped up beside them, the bill and a boxed pie in hand. Steve became aware that Don McLean was singing American Pie. "Is that song playing again?" he asked Libby. "Or is it just not over yet from before?"

"It is a long song, for sure," she laughed. "Even longer when it gets stuck in your head." She patted Steve's hand. "Enjoy the pie!"

CHAPTER FOURTEEN

Wonderful Life

Steve was preparing for his meetings to discuss the new sales compensation plan when his cell phone buzzed. It was Vance.

"Hi, Vance. I was just thinking about you. I'm starting discussions with my sales reps tomorrow about the new comp plan," Steve said. "I want to be able to give you a full report on how things went when we meet again in a few days.

"That's why I'm calling," Vance replied. "I'm not going to be able to meet you on our regular day and time."

"Oh," Steve said, unable to hide the surprise and disappointment in his voice. "Um, that's okay. We can certainly reschedule. Another day next week?"

"I'll have to let you know. I'm going to be out of town for at least a week, unfortunately. Our youngest daughter is a student at Florida Gulf Coast University in Fort Myers and her off-campus apartment was hit pretty hard by the recent hurricane down there. She's fine, but I'm going to go down and help get things back to some level of normalcy while she continues to attend classes. She's close to graduating with a degree in Entrepreneurship, and if she takes time off to tend to her living situation, it could impact her graduation and even some post-college opportunities she has lined up."

"I completely understand, Vance," Steve replied. "I'm so sorry she's going through that. She's lucky to have a dad like you to come to her aid."

"Thank you, Steve. And I'm lucky to have a job where I have some flexibility to put family first, and to have clients who understand that priority."

"Absolutely. Family before business. You know how I've struggled with that and how important it is for me to get back to that place in my own life. So, I totally support you in this."

"I appreciate that, Steve. I really do."

"As it turns out," Steve continued, "I'll need to take a day off soon to take Seth on a college visit. Hard to believe he's old enough, but it comes on quickly, doesn't it?"

"Sure does," Vance said. "I'll look forward to hearing about that. And I'll look forward to hearing how your comp plan meetings go, too."

"Thanks. I know you probably don't have much time, but do you have any last-minute advice before I brave those waters?" Steve asked.

Vance laughed. "You'll do fine, Steve. Just be resolute. Anticipate objections but remember that the actions you're taking and the plans you're setting in motion are essential not only to the survival of your company, but to the financial wellbeing of your employees and their families, as well."

"I know," Steve said. "Still, I expect some pushback."

"Encourage dialogue, of course, but don't waver in your convictions here. You must have each member of your sales team committed to your new direction going forward. Our strong desire is for Joe, Harry and Sally all to remain with your organization, but if they're unwilling to commit fully, you'll always be able to find skilled salespeople and train them on your product line. Remember our discussion about the importance of sales skills over industry or product knowledge?"

"Yes, I do."

Although it's certainly not our desired course of action to make any personnel changes, it's always a fallback option. Don't discuss that option upfront, naturally, but keep it in mind if the pushback becomes too severe."

"I understand."

"Another thing here, too, Steve. You will very likely experience a phenomenon that takes place each time a new compensation plan is delivered. Your plan will be received both positively and negatively. We know the new comp plan is fair and it rewards the kind of performance you're seeking. Your best salespeople will make a lot more money under this plan and your weakest salespeople will make less. Your weakest salespeople won't make as much money because they will now have to find new customers and sell more of the most profitable software. They can no longer be paid handsomely for existing customer's revenue that renews each year – they have to actually work now. Your best salespeople, on the other hand, will think this new plan is the best thing that's ever happened to them, due to the much larger compensation they're now earning. The amazing thing is, it is the same plan!"

"Interesting," Steve said. "Do you think I'll gain a sense of their perspectives on the new plan after I present it to them?"

"Yes, I think that's likely. It may even fall in line with your ranking of your sales team. You'll gain key insights as they react to their new plan, both moments after you deliver it and, in the days, and weeks to come. It won't take long to see who is willing to commit fully. The bottom line, Steve, is that the actions you are taking can and will benefit everyone if they will work with you and with each other to hit your revenue targets and achieve your growth goals. True team players will realize that and do their part!"

"Thanks for that reminder, Vance. You are helping me steel my nerves for tomorrow's discussions. So, when are you heading to Florida?"

"In just a few hours. I've got the SUV loaded with everything I can think of because supplies might be hard to come by down there right now."

"Well, let me know if you need anything while you're gone," Steve said.

"Just prayers for now," Vance responded.

"You got 'em!"

"Thank you, Steve. I'll be in touch soon and will look forward to our next get-together at The Fork."

"Same here. Safe travels."

After a day of prepping for the sales compensation plan meetings the next day, Steve headed home a little late, but in time for dinner. The pizza delivery driver rang the bell minutes after Steve got home, while he was upstairs changing clothes. With no one having an extracurricular activity that evening, it was their first planned family movie night. Pizza and pajamas seemed appropriate.

As Amy doled out slices from three different varieties of pizza – each child got to pick their favorite type to order – Steve took a seat at the dining room table. Doing a fingertip drumroll on the table, he then asked Braden, their youngest son, what movie he had selected for the family to watch.

"It's a Wonderful Life," the boy responded.

Seth laughed out loud. "What? A Wonderful Life? That's a Christmas movie. It's not even close to Christmas time," he said, rolling his eyes.

Amy gave her teenage son a stern look as Steve spoke up: "That's an interesting choice, Bray, and we all love that movie. Why'd you pick that one for us to watch tonight?"

The younger boy scowled at his brother who scowled back. "Well, you were working when we watched it last Christmas Eve," he said to Steve. "So, it was an *almost* family movie night, but not quite because we weren't all here. Now we are."

Steve's heart felt like it was melting. He could feel tears welling in his eyes. He cleared his throat. "Then it's a perfect choice, buddy. And I'm very happy this will be the first of many family movie nights."

As they watched the movie – all cell phones turned off and placed in a box in the kitchen, and the kids munching popcorn – Steve did his best to focus. His mind wandered from time to time, thinking about the discussions to come tomorrow with his sales reps. But whenever his thoughts took him there, he would look at his kids, young Abby and Braden on the floor and Seth in the recliner. Family before business, he reminded himself.

But he also knew that everything he was now doing, with Vance's guidance, was intended to make things better not only for his own family, but for his employees and their families, too. And it occurred to him that it went even beyond that; by making his company more viable, he was ensuring their products and services would continue. And because they sold software that made their clients' businesses more efficient and successful, that software kept more people employed and provided for still *more* families. Like George Bailey in the movie they were watching, Steve realized the impact he and his company had on a grander scope. That made what he was doing – as difficult as much of it was – truly imperative.

Indeed, it was a wonderful life, but he needed to do everything he could to make sure it stayed that way.

CHAPTER FIFTEEN

The Worth of the Journey

The day after Steve met with his salespeople to discuss the new sales compensation plan, he and Seth set out on a long road trip to Bloomington, Indiana to visit Indiana University. It was a junior-year visit that high school students with post-secondary education aspirations were encouraged to take. Seth and his parents had chosen IU because it was home of the renowned Kelley School of Business – with many business major options to explore – as well as the storied IU swim program. Although it was uncertain if he could gain a scholarship at a big program like IU, he was cautiously optimistic that Seth could lower his times in his senior year to a level worthy of at least a small scholarship.

Unfortunately, Amy was unable to join them, having made a prior commitment to chaperone Abby's class on a field trip to the zoo. Even though Steve would have loved for Amy to tour the hilly and sprawling IU campus with him and Seth, he was also grateful for some one-on-one time with his son.

His hopes of Seth being more talkative than normal were not initially realized as Seth often needed to be prompted into conversation, usually replying with short answers: "Taking Mia to prom again this year?" *Maybe.* "Are you considering on-campus residence hall living, an off-campus apartment, or maybe even a frat house?" *Probably dorm.* "Are you more nervous or excited about going to college next year?" *Excited, I guess.* "Any worries?" *Not really. Not yet, anyway.* "Have you thought of questions to ask during the visit today?" *A few, but mostly I'll play it by ear.*

And on and on. Still, it was good, and Steve knew that times like this were becoming more scarce and thus, more precious.

The visit went well, with Seth much more talkative and downright impressive as he interacted with his tour guide Jawaan and the faculty and coaches he was able to chat with briefly. It was a nice day to walk the rolling hills of downtown among the campus buildings with their strong facades of limestone culled from local quarries. They had lunch in a dining hall; and Seth even got to take a few laps in the water at the Counsilman Billingsley Aquatics Center.

A long day, but a good one.

As the sun began to set, Steve recognized an exit on their way home that would lead him to The Fork if he took it. He was tempted. Ultimately, however, he stayed on the highway, passing up the opportunity for pie (if any was left in the evening) along with a visit with Libby and the crew. He and Seth were both tired, still far from home, and a trip to The Fork would essentially hijack a day focused on Seth, Steve thought. Besides that, he didn't know if Libby would still be working into the evening. He hoped not, frankly, for she needed home time, too. Family time. Everyone did. As that thought played in his mind, it occurred to Steve that neither Vance nor Libby spoke much about life beyond The Fork. He knew little of their private lives, of their families. As friendly and sociable as they were, they always managed to steer conversations back to Steve and *his* family. He supposed that's why they were successful, at least in part. Vance and Libby clearly had servant attitudes and were generous in their focus on Steve. He admired them greatly.

As it grew darker and the highways continued to stretch out before them, Steve noticed that Seth had grown quieter than normal. No longer was he talking about the day's events, no requests for restroom stops, no voice dictations as he texted his best friend, Jake. His kid – the young man beside him – had fallen asleep.

Steve looked at his son and started to reminisce about how quickly Seth had grown up: he couldn't believe he would be going off to college soon. As he looked at him now, slouched in the passenger seat, he also began to picture in his mind how Seth had been as a newborn, then as a toddler splashing in a pool, as a kid playing T-ball and basketball and soccer, as a prize winner in the Science Fair, and as a compassionate young man collecting change for the homeless and donating his time to greenspace cleanup projects each year. Steve realized how proud he was of the person beside him and thankful he and Amy had been able to give him some good solid foundations. Of course, thoughts like this reminded him that his own foundations were currently on shaky ground.

His mind wandered back to the sales compensation plan meetings he had held off-site with his sales team members. Vance's guidance had bolstered him with the resolve he needed to stand firm and be confident when presenting the new plan. Still, as expected, each salesperson had a different reaction.

Sally, still learning her role, was the most accepting. She could see that the changes could benefit her because she was still in the mode of targeting new customers, as opposed to earning compensation based largely on retaining current customers in her portfolio.

Joe was cautiously optimistic about the new plan, though he worried about short-term hits to his income as he switched focus toward new customers and the more profitable product line.

Harry, as feared, didn't like the new plan. At all! It was, after all, *change,* and Harry didn't like change. He saw no problem with the way things were because he was profiting handsomely – or at least comfortably – under the current plan. The new plan would mean less money from current customers and that meant more work attempting to land new ones. He said he understood the changes from the big-picture company perspective but couldn't quite remove himself for very long from the scope of what the changes meant for him and his situation.

Steve could empathize with Harry and with the smaller concerns Joe and Sally had voiced. Change wasn't a comfortable thing, even if it ultimately benefited everyone. He had done his best to present the important and necessary facets of the plan as it related to their potential to make more money, but only time would tell if all three salespeople would get on board.

Steve knew he had his work cut out for him and that it would be a long road ahead. But as he turned his eyes from the highway revealed before him in the beams of his headlights and looked again at his son, Steve was more certain than ever in the worth of the journey.

CHAPTER SIXTEEN

Purpose and Direction

A week and a half later, Steve and Vance were finally able to get back together at The Fork. As he stepped inside, the smell of the bacon and the coffee and the pies enveloped him like a warm embrace. And when Libby and Vance – and even Bobthecook and Jukebox Jack – called out his name, it felt like coming home.

"Be with you in a minute, Buddy," Libby called from the far end of the counter. Steve saluted her and shook Vance's hand when he reached the corner booth.

"Welcome back," Vance said.

"Thank you; same to you," Steve replied. "I hope everything went well with your daughter and your Florida trip."

"Well, yes, things went fine. She was happy to see us and to have some help getting back to normal. Still a handful of minor things for her to deal with, but she's on top of it now. I suppose it's good that our kids handle certain things on their own. Gives them confidence, don't you think? A rite of passage and all that."

Steve nodded in agreement. "It's hard letting go and letting them make their own way, but if we do our jobs well, they are up to the task, right?"

"Absolutely."

"Looks like you got a little bit of sun while you were there. Were you able to find a beach and relax for a bit?"

Vance added a splash of creamer to his coffee. "A little bit, on the last day there. Of course, we were often in and out of the sun, cleaning and shopping and repairing and replacing. Strange how much sun there was in the aftermath of the storm. Hurricanes are hard to prepare for and recover from in the best of circumstances, but our daughter and her friends got off pretty easy in the grand scheme of things."

Coffee pot in hand and looking like she, too had gotten some sun since Steve had seen her last, Libby appeared. She leaned in and gave him a one-shoulder hug. "Glad to have you back, young man," she said cheerily, reaching and filling his coffee cup."

"Glad to be back. You know, Libby, you should really bottle the smells in this place and sell it as cologne or at least as home air freshener."

"Never!" Libby exclaimed. "If we did that, people would just stay home, and we'd lose all our business!"

Steve stirred his coffee to dissipate some heat. "I think people come here for the food and the company. The smells are like icing on the cake," he said.

Libby laughed.

"And speaking of cake," Steve continued, "what is the pie du jour?"

"Oh, honey, it's another good'n. Peachy Keen Beachy Pie this week, in honor of, well ya know…."

"Let me guess," Steve ventured, "it's a peach pie with a sugar-coated crust to represent a beach?"

Libby high-fived him and laughed. "Pretty soon you'll be in charge of pie planning here. Back in a jiffy!"

Steve looked back at Vance, noticing not only the tan but also the warm smile on his face as his eyes followed Libby away from the table. "I'll tell you, Vance, this is such a pleasant, homey kind of place that I'm tempted to set up shop and work from here!"

Vance laughed, but nodded in agreement. "I'm lucky to be able to do that from time to time, mixing business with pleasure." He pushed his coffee cup aside and added, "So, the last time we spoke, you were going to talk to your sales team members about the new compensation plan. I've been on pins and needles waiting to hear how that went, but first, tell me about your college trip with your son. Did you do that yet?"

"Yes, late last week, the day after the sales team comp plan talks, actually. The trip was a good one. My son is not very talkative – keeps a lot to himself. In that sense, Vance, he reminds me of you. Kind of a quiet strength forming there, I think. But it was a good day and I think he's decided to go to IU and to work hard to boost his standings in both academics and athletics."

"That's outstanding! Sounds like he knows where he's going, and that his new sense of destination will also fuel him with a serious sense of purpose and direction."

Steve laughed. "Ah, a metaphorical segue to the business at hand if ever there was one!"

Vance smiled. "You're a quick study, Steve. Okay, so, down to business…"

But first Libby returned, took their orders and dashed away again.

"Okay, where were we?" Vance asked. "Oh, yes, you were about to tell me about your sales team and the comp plan meetings. So, how did your introduction of the new compensation plan go?"

"Well, as we suspected, my team reacted in different ways. Sally liked it and it seemed to energize her because she could see more opportunity. Joe is cautiously optimistic, but Harry didn't like it at all really."

"What didn't Harry like about the new plan?"

"He thought he would have to work harder to make the same amount of money."

"Will he?"

"I suppose so," Steve said. "He won't be able to make the same amount of money without driving new revenue."

"But if he does drive new revenue, he could make even more money, right?"

"Yes, that's true. That's the way the new plan is designed."

"Does Harry realize that?"

"I think he does, but he is focusing on the negative."

"And does that surprise you about Harry?"

Steve sighed. "No, unfortunately, that's pretty consistent with how he typically acts."

Vance shifted in his seat. "And if I may hazard a guess here… in the past, if he complained loud enough, Harry got his way, right?"

Steve nodded and sheepishly pursed his lips. "Yes, I usually surrendered to his demands."

Vance smiled. "Well, you have the newly discovered power of self-awareness, Steve. But this is the start of a new day and Harry will learn that he needs to comply with your expectations or you'll find someone that does. We'd obviously prefer he stay – after all, Harry embracing the plan is the quickest path to success for you – but you need to be prepared to move on to a new sales rep if he doesn't."

"I agree, I can't continue doing things the same way anymore – it just doesn't work, and it undermines team motivation and the entire culture."

"Ah, very good. Again, very self-aware. Your old leadership style wasn't getting you where you want to go – where you *need* to go – so it has to change. What I want you to appreciate and be able to share with your team when necessary, Steve, is that you're not only asking your team members to make uncomfortable changes; you are demanding change within yourself, too."

"True enough," said Steve.

"And as I mentioned during our phone call before your meetings, the new comp plan is the same for everyone, even if some reps view it positively while others view it negatively.

"That's what I discovered."

Vance continued. "And remember this: it is a *fair* plan – one that allows the best performers to make more money and the poor performers to make less money. And assuming it incents the behavior you want, you'll find it separates your future stars from those who are unwilling, or unable, to take that next step, even if it's in their best interest. In any case, that's what you want, right?"

"That is *definitely* what I want."

Libby delivered steaming plates of food and dashed away again. While the two men let the food cool a bit before digging in, Vance carried on. "So, did you also start your weekly meetings with each member of your sales team?"

"Yes, I did, and that was interesting, too."

"How so?"

Steve picked up a forkful of eggs and blew on it before speaking. "Well, I did as you suggested and asked each person to come prepared to discuss each new opportunity they're working on, including the type of opportunity, deal amount, stage of the sales process it is in, and when they think it will close. I also asked them to consider anything I can do to help them."

"What observations did you make from their responses?" Vance asked before finally starting to eat his breakfast.

"I noticed that they made a lot of assumptions," Steve said.

"Tell me more about that. What do you mean?"

"Well, when I asked them direct questions about the prospective customer's state of mind, needs, objections, and what is slowing down their sales process, all of their feedback was their opinion or their gut reaction or just a *sense* they had. None of their feedback was directly from the prospective customer."

"Why do you suppose that was?"

"I don't know," Steve admitted. "I suppose they never asked them directly to get their questions answered."

Vance sipped his coffee. "I think you're on to something, Steve. It's difficult to take action based on what you *think* you know, rather than what you *know* you know. Salespeople often don't take the obvious first step, and that step is to simply ask the question. You see, there's no judgment in a question – a question is just a question. I've often had sales reps tell me they don't know if the prospective customer will answer their question, and my reply is, 'How could you find out?' Of course, they typically respond with, 'I guess I could just ask them.'"

Steve chuckled. "That's so obvious, of course, so why don't most of us just ask what we want to know?"

Vance hesitated a moment. "We often throw our own obstacle in our path and then wonder how it got there. Sales is an honorable profession, Steve – it is trying to fill a prospective client's need. If you can do that, both parties benefit – it is the purest definition of a 'win-win.' Think of it this way: In its most noble essence, sales isn't about trying to get someone to buy something they don't need – that's what some salespeople do, and it gives us all a bad reputation. Rather, it's our job to find out *if* we can help the prospective customer, to genuinely try to find out if we can fill a need. If we can, that's great. If we can't, we have to walk away and perhaps even steer them in a different direction, a *better* direction toward a true solution for their needs. Our job is to serve *them*, not serve ourselves. By serving others, you will also be rewarded."

"I like that a lot," Steve said. "I need to keep that in mind and make sure my salespeople adopt that as a guiding principle, too."

"Excellent!" Vance exclaimed. "So, what else did you find out during your weekly meetings?"

"Well, I learned that each sales rep has a different view of when a prospective customer should receive a proposal. And even their optimism for closing a sale was very different."

"Tell me more about the proposal portion first," Vance said.

"It appears that Harry offers to provide a proposal really early in the process, Joe very late in the process, and Sally in-between."

"What criteria did each use to determine when a proposal was given?"

"Well," Steve said, "that appears to be the issue; they didn't use any criteria, they seemed to move forward with a proposal based only on when it felt right."

"Felt right?"

"Yes, when they *thought* it was needed. There was no consistency within each rep's territory, and certainly not across reps."

Vance leaned in. "Ah, yes, I suppose that was to be expected. The good news is that we can fix that."

Libby made a stop at the table. "Need anything else right now, gents?" She was already topping off the coffee.

"Nothing else for me, thanks," Vance said. Steve waived her off, too. The men took several bites, their food fully cooled now.

"Now," Vance said, "how about those differing levels of optimism you mentioned?"

"Well, I wanted to get an idea of how much revenue would come in over the next few months, and to match that up with the two-year sales forecast you had me put together. What I discovered was that Harry and Joe are overly optimistic and Sally is too pessimistic."

"And how did you determine that, Steve?"

"When I asked detailed questions about whether they were talking to the ultimate decision maker or if there was budget money set aside to pay for our software or what the decision-making process was, they didn't know most of the time. They simply, well, they just *guessed*."

"I see. And why do you suppose Sally was so pessimistic about the probability of closing her deals?"

Steve stared at the pattern on the table. "I thought about that, Vance, and I believe it's my fault. You see, when I told her it sounded to me like it was more likely she would close some of these deals, she said, 'I know you don't want me to be wrong on my predictions, so I'm trying to be really conservative.'"

Vance smiled. "Really conservative. Interesting."

Steve continued. "So, I realized it all stemmed from a meeting a few months ago, when cash flow was really poor. Sally thought a deal was going to close, but it didn't, and I got really upset with her. It was probably the strongest I've been with her since she's been with the company. I was just frustrated because of the company's poor cash flow. But I think I reacted too strongly and I gave her the impression that I didn't want her real forecast. So, in the end, I think I caused her to only tell me when a deal was going to close, when it is almost 100% done."

"I see."

"The other day, I told her I want her to be realistic and not overly conservative or cautious. Still, I think she's hesitant because of our earlier interaction."

Vance cleared his throat. "Steve, as I see it, your advice to her on being realistic is sound. And I'm confident you can recover from that one meeting and help all your reps be more accurate when forecasting future deals. We just need to help you build a consistent sales process, as well as a tool to monitor and project future revenue."

"That sounds good."

"I was taught by Charlie many years ago," Vance said, "that you can miss your quota or you can miss your forecast, but you can't miss both."

Steve frowned. "I'm not quite sure what you mean."

"Well, you don't want to miss the quota assigned to you, but not knowing you are going to miss your quota – meaning your sales forecast was too high – isn't allowable either. In the end, you missed your quota and you didn't know it was going to happen. Look at it this way: The company is counting on each sales rep to know their sales pipeline well enough to help their manager understand what is going to happen. If too many reps miss their quota without knowing it was going to happen, expenditures are going to be out of line with revenue. The company may have made purchases based on predicted revenue, but now that is out of alignment.

"You see, Steve, being too pessimistic can be as bad as being too optimistic. Being too pessimistic might lead you to not invest in the business enough, because you didn't realize revenue would be higher. But creating a defined sales process and putting tools in place to make forecasting future revenue more accurate, along with the conversations you have weekly with each of your reps, will lead to accurate forecasts you can depend on."

"I'm all for that, so how do I make that happen?"

"Glad you asked," Vance said. "That leads to this week's homework. What I want you to do is document your sales cycle. In other words, document each possible step your reps could take when progressing through a sale. Feel free to include your sales team in this exercise. Pick their brains. Just write down what you do at each step, and we can discuss what you put together when we meet next week."

"Okay," Steve said. "Sounds like it could get complicated."

"Well, Steve, you can't overhaul or fine tune a process you don't understand, so detail is important."

As if on cue, Libby came back. "And this is important, too, Steve. Do you want a whole Peachy Keen Beachy Pie to take home or just a slice to enjoy here?"

CHAPTER SEVENTEEN
Pie It Forward

After she cleared the dishes and Steve left, Libby joined Vance in the corner booth. As soon as she sat, her phone chimed behind the counter. At the same time, Vance's phone chirped.

"I'll check mine in a few," Libby said. "Go ahead and check yours if you want."

Vance unlocked his screen and tapped it a few times. "She passed her exams," he shared, and then read the text verbatim: *Passed! Can't thank you enough for coming to my rescue and working so hard so I could focus. Love ya bunches. Will call later. xoxo*

"Oh, that's great news!" Libby cried. "Makes it all worthwhile, doesn't it?"

"Yes, indeed," Vance said. "Sure does."

"Then again, that's what parents do, right? And it's what we do in our jobs, too, eh, sweetie?"

Vance smiled at her. "Serving others, you mean? Helping them have better days?"

Libby nodded. "Mmm hmm. I guess we here at The Fork help the breakfast crowd get a good start on the day to come, all right. But what you do, Vance, is probably even more special because it helps people like Steve have better days for years to come."

Vance looked away briefly, staring out the window.

Libby patted his hand. "Oh, I know, I know. It's not about you and it's not about you getting any real recognition for what you do; it's that ol' 'goodness is its own reward' thing, right?"

"You got it," Vance said. "Then again, I'm no Saint – I still cash those paychecks from my clients. All except Steve, of course."

"Well, you're getting free breakfasts with that one, and making a real difference for him and his company and his family, too." The counter bell dinged, and Libby rose from the booth. "Saint Vance or not, I'm proud of you."

Steve had two full pies resting on the passenger-side floorboard of the car as he headed home – one for the family, the other for his sales team. He knew he was asking his reps to make big changes and leave their comfort zones. More than that, he was asking them to take a leap of faith in themselves and in him, in his new style and tone of leadership. He was sure he hadn't truly inspired his reps to greatness so far, so it was understandable if they were a bit skeptical – or in the case of Harry, a lot skeptical – for now. So, the pie for his sales reps wasn't so much a peace offering or a bribe as it was a way to "pie it forward" for their efforts to come.

As a light rain fell, and as the diner grew more distant and his office grew closer, Steve reflected on the many changes he had made so far. Not just changes to the compensation plan or even to his comprehension of the scope of the problems facing his company. No, most of the changes had been to his worldview. With Vance's help, he was now seeing things more clearly and more hopefully. Hope was a miraculous thing, he thought. Merely planting that seedling of hope that his future could be better than the recent past was helping his better self take root – the better self that was a kinder person and a stronger leader at work and at home. He aspired now to make a difference for others, but more than that, he also wanted to model, with his life and his actions, the kinds of behaviors he hoped those around him would model also. The prospect of inspiring others to become their better selves was intoxicating, a headier concoction than any drink or any drug, he thought.

It occurred to him, though, that it would also be easy to get too full of himself. That the successes he now *expected* could bring a danger of overconfidence, of cockiness, of arrogance. That he could somehow diminish the influence of Vance and of his family. That he could lose sight of how easy it is to fall, to falter, to fail.

Of how close he had come to losing everything.

As he drove, Steve resolved not only to do the hard work necessary to succeed, but to stay humble and helpful to others in the process. And although he didn't know if he could ever be as inspirational as his beneficent teacher at The Fork, let alone as inspirational as Charlie had been for Vance before him, Steve was determined to try.

The rain let up and a few miles later a chime sounded. His gas tank was nearing empty. Although he could probably drive another 30 miles or more before running the tank dry, Steve knew that exits were few and far between along this stretch of road; so, he took the next one and pulled into the gas station just to the right. As he filled the tank, he noticed the restaurant across the road. It was the same one where he had stopped at the drive-thru the last time. With his tank full and feeling a bit thirsty again, Steve drove across the road and parked in the lot. He went in and used the restroom and then stepped to the counter.

He recognized the girl immediately. She was the one who had been working the drive-up window last time. He smiled and ordered a soft drink and noticed that the girl kept watching him as she rang up the order.

When he handed her a $50 bill again, her face lit up. "Did you come through the drive-thru a while back and pay with a fifty?"

Steve nodded. "I believe I did, yes."

"And did you ask me to pay for the order of the family in the car behind you?"

"That rings a bell, too," Steve said.

The cashier grinned an almost radiant smile, her face practically flowing into an expression of warmth and gratitude. "I did as you asked," she said. "I told the lady you had paid for her order. She could hardly hear me at first because her kids were screaming, and she seemed like they were on her last nerve. So, I repeated myself and she seemed confused for a moment, but then it was, well, it was a beautiful thing…"

"What's that?"

"The lady started to cry. Right there at my window, she burst into tears, just very grateful, very humbled, too, I think."

"Thank you for sharing that with me," Steve said.

"There's more, though," the cashier said. Steve looked behind himself, making sure he was not holding up any other customers. The dining room was virtually empty. There was no one in line.

The cashier continued. "I had noticed that the woman in the car had only ordered a single large drink and a single large French fry. All those kids and that's all she ordered. I was pretty sure she would have ordered more if she could have, so I filled a bag with burgers and fries and added some boxes of apple juice to the order."

"That was very thoughtful of you, very perceptive and kind," Steve said. "I hope you took the rest of the cost of that extra food out of the fifty."

"No sir," the cashier said. "I took care of it. Your kindness and your generosity inspired me, I guess."

Steve felt a lump in his throat.

"I gave the lady in the car your $50 bill as 'change' for her order," the young woman said. "I hope that was okay."

Steve shuffled on his feet and bit his lip to quell the rising emotion. "It was more than okay," he said. "It was the perfect thing to do. Thank you for doing that."

The cashier blinked back a tear of her own. She handed Steve his drink cup for the self-serve drink machine. He nodded and started to walk away.

"Wait, sir, you forgot your change."

"Keep it," Steve said. Lost in thoughts of gratitude, he filled his cup till it ran over.

CHAPTER EIGHTEEN

The Student

It was nearly two weeks before Steve and Vance were able to reconvene at The Fork. Vance had been catching up on client work that had accumulated while he was in Florida; and Steve took advantage of the extra time to more proactively meet with – and travel with – his sales reps. Just as he had been tempted to bring Seth to The Fork after their Indiana University day visit, Steve had also been tempted to bring his sales reps to the diner. There was a part of him that suspected that all who entered this place would be swept up in its wonders, charmed not only by its sounds, its smells, its people and pies, but also by the magic of possibility.

But there was another part of Steve that feared bringing others here. What if they just saw it as an ordinary old greasy spoon hangout? What if they weren't as charmed by Libby? As captivated by the music on the jukebox? As *transported* by the diner's 1950s nostalgic American ambience? What if they simply weren't in the same psychological headspace in need of that kind of transformation as Steve had been?

Steve didn't know if the transformation was due to the nostalgia at The Fork, its employees, Vance or just Steve himself, but he felt like people everywhere probably need a little more of what The Fork offers. It's almost like the "land that time forgot," he thought, and being transported back to a simpler time seemed to be just what he needed.

As he neared the diner, Steve realized he was probably overthinking the whole thing. Still, he doubted his kids or his sales team members could truly appreciate the magic of The Fork the way he did. Maybe they were lucky in that sense, because they didn't *need* that kind of magic, at least not yet. Needing it, he supposed, was his special burden right here and right now.

But when he entered the diner this day, in place of magic was fighting. *Everybody was Kung Fu fighting…*

Carl Douglas was playing on the jukebox, and throughout the diner heads were bobbing to the beat. An interesting place, to be sure.

"Ah, Steve, welcome back!" Libby called from behind the counter. She put down her dry-erase marker and turned the signboard. Pie of the day was Grasshopper Pie! "This one is kind of a tribute to you, sweetie."

"Okay-y-y," Steve said, "not sure I follow what you—"

"Maybe I can explain." It was Vance. He had stepped up next to Steve. They shook hands. "Sometimes, Libby refers to my clients as grasshoppers."

Steve shook his head, still not making the connection.

"Does the music give you a clue?" Libby asked?

"Kung Fu Fighting and grasshoppers…" Steve mused. "Wait a minute, wasn't there an old TV show where—"

"You got it!" Libby exclaimed.

"The old Kung Fu series," Vance interjected. "David Carradine played the main character, called Caine. As a child, he had a teacher, a master if you will, named Po, and Po called him 'Grasshopper.' Kind of synonymous with his student because of that."

Steve chuckled. "I vaguely – very vaguely – remember something about that. Just how old *are* you people anyway?"

"Watch it, buster!" Libby boomed. Vance laughed, and the two men took their stations in the corner booth.

Libby filled their coffee cups and glared at Steve. "How old are you people…" she repeated. "Old enough to teach you a thing or two, *grasshopper!*" She cackled, gave him a tap on the shoulder and darted away.

"She's a good sport," Steve said.

Vance nodded in agreement. "I think she's mastered the art of not taking herself too seriously. Helps her keep things in perspective, I suppose."

"Good lesson for all of us, right?"

"So, Grasshopper – okay, that's the last time I'll call you that – how have things gone since we last got together?"

"They've gone well," Steve said. "I applied what we discussed last time and my meetings with the sales reps were much more productive."

"Have you been able to travel with each of your reps yet?"

"Yes, and although it's taking up some of my time, I can see where I'm able to make an impact on them. I think that will lead to them being able to handle most of these deals without my direct involvement."

"So, a short-term investment will lead to a long-term gain?"

"Yes, I believe so."

"I do, too, Steve. I have a feeling that, while you might be the student here, you are the master for your sales reps. I've always found that can be not only gratifying, but confidence building, too."

"I think you're right," Steve said. "I never thought of it that way, but it does feel that way in practice."

"And I think, Steve, as you continue along this path, and your sales reps are able to take ownership of situations, their confidence will grow as well. Success breeds success, you know."

Libby was hovering, waiting for Vance to finish, before taking their orders. She winked at Steve, as if needing to let him know she wasn't offended by his age reference, and then dashed away to place the order ticket on the carousel for Bobthecook.

"So, then, how did your follow-up discussions go with each rep and their understanding of the compensation plans?" Vance asked.

"Well, I learned that although they signed the new compensation plan claiming they understood the plan, they didn't all understand it as well as I thought they did."

"Did you have further discussions about the plan then? Do your reps understand it better now?"

"Yes," Steve said. "I clarified points where they'd demonstrated a lack of understanding, and then questioned them in enough detail to make sure they got it. I'm certain they truly grasp the plan now."

"Okay, that's great. Taking that additional step to ensure understanding is also a short-term investment with a long-term gain," Vance said. "Let's move on to the steps in the sales process you put together. Walk me through what you've put together."

With the table not yet cluttered by food, Steve laid out some pages and walked Vance through the fundamental sales process, step by step.

Vance listened and nodded and made some notes in his own notebook. When Steve had finished, Vance was starting to give Steve his feedback when he saw Jenny carrying a tray laden with their breakfasts.

"Libby is taking a load off for a couple minutes," Jenny said. She placed syrup on the table and extra napkins. "You fellas need anything else right now?"

Steve and Vance looked at one another and then Vance said, "I think you've got it covered, Jen. Thank you."

The younger woman smiled and stepped away.

"Looks like Libby has trained her own grasshopper well," Steve said.

"I think you're right, Steve. Grasshoppers are everywhere, it seems."

Each man took a couple of bites before Vance continued: "Steve, I would like to share something with you. It's something I noticed as you explained your process—"

"Please do."

Vance sipped his coffee and went on, saying, "I've found it typical with most business owners that their sales processes are missing something. Many of them, just like you, have relied on reactive buying. What I mean by that is that they've produced wonderful products or services for many years; and this excellence has led to many warm leads and often significant revenue. That's all great, of course, and has sustained their businesses for years. But suddenly a tipping point occurs where that excellence is no longer enough to drive sufficient revenue. In your case, Steve, competition is one of the key factors.

"And now you, like these other business owners, have to turn to *proactive* selling. Unfortunately, because you haven't had to engage in this type of sales, your team doesn't have the understanding, and perhaps not even the capabilities or necessary skills, to sell proactively with a high level of success. So, ultimately, those steps get left out of the process. And because of this, other key steps get left out that would make the sales process even more effective, too."

Steve looked concerned.

"Like I said," Vance continued, "it's typical of businesses in your situation. And it is correctable, of course. So, Steve, tell me what happens when a warm lead doesn't come to you and you need to reach out and proactively have a conversation with a prospective customer?"

Steve swallowed a bite of pancake and shrugged his shoulders. "Well, we don't do that much, I guess. We've always responded to leads that have come in, but that isn't happening as often these days. In hindsight, I guess that's been true for a few years now."

"So, we see the root of the problem," Vance said. "And I think you can also see that the process you've set out here for us to review is only part of the overall process you may need to use."

"Yes, I see that now," Steve said. "Can you help me fill in the gaps and understand, well, *how to sell?*"

Vance nodded, and for the next fifteen minutes the men ate, asked and answered questions, and made notes. Vance walked Steve through the traditional steps in a proactive sales process and helped him fill in what was missing with his current process.

Vance asked next about specific activities and actions necessary at each step in the sales cycle in order to move to the next step. For the reactive process he originally proposed, Steve explained what would need to happen at each step.

"Can you see how validating what would need to happen at each sales cycle step before moving to the next step would bring consistency to your sales forecasting?" Vance asked.

"Yes," Steve said. "It would ensure that what I had happen with the proposals given by each rep in the past doesn't happen in the future. They could only issue a proposal when certain activities were crossed off as having been completed by the prospective customer, as well as the rep."

"That's correct," Vance said. "Now let's talk about what probability of closure will take place at each of these steps." Steve shared his thoughts on how likely the eventual closure of the sale was at each step. His projections made Vance smile knowingly.

"Steve," he said, "I thought you might have those views about closure rates by step. You see, business owners who haven't proactively sold for a long time usually estimate the probability of closure too high – meaning they are used to dealing with prospective clients that have heard great things about their product or service and are very likely to buy. Unfortunately, this is quite different when talking to a prospective customer that has never heard of your company or product."

Together, the men made notes, giving Steve more information for more realistically projecting closure rates at each step.

"Next time, Steve, I would also like you to tell me more about the Customer Relationship Management software you purchased," Vance noted.

Steve raised his head and locked eyes again with Vance. "Well, as I mentioned some time ago, we bought one but don't use it. Never have. I guess we just got so locked into doing things the way we always have that we never got around to installing it."

"I see," Vance said, his voice devoid of judgment or nuance.

"Ironic, isn't it?" Steve mused. "Here we are a software company promoting the benefits and even the necessity of utilizing software to optimize operations and we haven't even taken that step ourselves."

Vance leaned back. He took a sip of coffee and said quietly, "Okay, I lied. I'm going to call you Grasshopper again." With that, he leaned forward once more. "Grasshopper, seek first to know your own journey's beginning and end."

"Sounds like a quote."

"Well, I may have watched my share of Kung Fu episodes and learned a bit of Master Po's wisdom."

"So, Master Vance, what do you mean by knowing the journey's beginning and end?"

"Well, it has obvious, if elusive meanings, of course, for the life journey or even the definable sales processes we have been discussing," Vance explained. "But with regard to a CRM, if you have a good one, properly configured to your needs, it can help you know the path and understand where you are on the journey from first contact to conversion and even through client account management."

"You are wise, indeed, Master," Steve said.

Vance laughed. "Okay, so let's talk more about CRMs next time. Also, bring back for me the updated and fully documented sales process information, with activities at each sales process step, along with your updated probabilities of closure."

"I sure will."

Steve looked over his shoulder just as Libby swooped in with the check in hand. She also carried a bite of Grasshopper Pie on a fork. As Steve tasted it, his eyes practically rolling back in his head with delight, Libby snatched up empty breakfast plates and said, "I'll box up that pie for you, Grasshopper."

CHAPTER NINETEEN

The Wizard

After being on the road into the evening several nights recently, Steve was determined to make it home in time for dinner and another family movie night; this time his daughter Abby was making the choice as part of her week-long 11th birthday celebration.

He was clearing off his desktop – something he'd tried to be more diligent about lately – when his cell phone rang. He grimaced, fearing it was a work-related distraction that would threaten his evening plans.

It was Vance.

"Just checking in on you, Steve," he said. "I know it's late in the day and I won't keep you, but I wanted you to know I'm available in case you have any questions between now and our next get-together."

"I appreciate that, Vance. I really do."

"You are into the heavy-lifting phase of things," Vance said, the cell connection breaking up slightly. "I'm asking a lot of you as you fine-tune your sales process and think about your CRM. Just curious if you've had much time to deal with that and if you have any questions or are running into any roadblocks."

Steve quietly straightened up some papers and answered, "I think I'm doing okay for now. I'm probably running a little bit behind, but nothing motivates like a deadline, eh?"

Vance laughed. "That's very true. At least for me."

"The call is breaking up a bit, Vance. Are you on the road?"

"Yes, sorry about that. If we lose the connection, there's no need to call me back unless you have anything specific to discuss. I try to make follow-up calls when on the road as long as I believe I won't have to write anything down."

"Good idea," Steve said. "Just drive safely."

"Always hands-free if I call from the road," Vance said.

"Too bad business can't be more hands-free more of the time," Steve mused.

"Well now, that's what we're aiming for, right?" Vance asked. "By setting up new systems and processes, it should free you up to lead your business rather than being involved in the day-to-day details."

"Sounds good to me."

"Well, again, just checking to see if you had any immediate concerns as you dial in your processes."

"Not really. Not yet, anyway," Steve said. "I'm meeting individually with Harry, Joe and Sally tomorrow to involve them in the process, to get their insights and buy-in."

More crackling in the connection. "...wise, Steve. ...good to get your team on board."

"I'll give you a full report when we reconvene at The Fork," Steve said. "I really do appreciate—" And with that, a click that told Steve the connection was lost.

Connection. It occurred to Steve that his student/mentor connection with Vance was strong and getting stronger. There was real trust between them. Steve trusted Vance to help him find his way, and Vance was trusting Steve to make things work.

That thought tempted Steve to take work home, but he knew that this was not the night to be distracted. He needed to get home and be "present" with his family all evening. It was Abby's movie night, their *family* night. Such moments mattered more than just about anything Steve did these days.

This time Steve met the pizza delivery driver in the driveway.

"One pepperoni, extra *extra* pepperoni, actually. Also, one veggie with barbecue sauce, and one pizza with hamburger and chicken," the driver said. "Interesting, um, choices."

"Weird kids," Steve said. He handed the driver enough for the pizzas and a nice tip.

Inside, after changing into sweatpants and his robe – loungewear required for pizza-and-pajamas-family-movie-night – Steve joined Amy and the kids in the Family Room. They had decided to further relax normal etiquette by eating in front of the TV while they watched the movie.

"So, Abbs, you're the theater owner tonight. What movie are we screening?" Steve asked his daughter.

Abby produced a piece of paper with a picture drawn on it. "See if you can figure it out," she said.

Steve studied the drawing. Abby had drawn a girl with pig tails and a small dog walking together down a curvy road that she had colored in yellow marker.

Steve shouldn't have been surprised by her selection, given that his daughter tended to be an old soul, always picking a classic movie over a current movie that most other 11-year-olds might select. "Hmmm," he teased, "whatever could it be?"

Braden looked over his dad's shoulder. "Wizard the Boss!" he exclaimed.

Seth rolled his eyes. "My gosh, Bray, it's not "Wizard the Boss," it's Wizard *of Oz.*"

"Ah, and another family movie night tradition emerges," Amy said, glaring at her sons.

Steve laughed and turned to Abby. "Assuming we are watching *The Wizard of Oz*, why did you choose that one?"

"I chose it because you call me 'Munchkin' a lot, so I like the Munchkins in the movie. And the dog – I like Toto, too. And Dorothy, of course, and—"

"I like Professor Marvel," Seth interrupted. "He doesn't have to share a house with anyone."

"Alright, alright," Steve said, "let's start down the yellow brick road."

When the movie was over, even though it was late for a school night, Steve started another new tradition. He asked each family member for their opinion. "What did you each like best about the movie?"

"I liked it when the movie went from kinda brown looking to super colorful," Braden said. "That was awesome!"

"I liked it when they melted the witch," Seth added. "Although I think that explains why she was so mean since she could never go swimming." He cocked his head slightly. "I wonder if it gave her heartburn to drink a glass of water, though?"

Amy shook her head. "Abby, what about you?" she asked. "You picked the movie. What did you like best?"

"I liked it that Dorothy had a dog," Abby said. "A young girl needs a dog, I think."

"Oh, boy, I had a feeling we'd get to that before the night was done," Steve laughed.

Amy spoke up next. "I liked that Dorothy ended up in her own home and her own bed, just like where other people I know need to be."

Steve laughed. "Oh, Ames, you are such a *mom!*"

The kids started up the stairs to their rooms. Suddenly, Abby yelled, "Wait! Daddy didn't tell us what *he* liked about the movie."

All eyes turned to Steve. After a moment of reflection, he said, "Well, I think I liked the journey. They were all on a journey – a quest you might call it – and they knew where they needed to go and learned how to get there. And even though there were challenges along the way, they made it because they were in it together." He smiled. "Yeah, sometimes it's the journey that matters most."

CHAPTER TWENTY

Tin Roof Pie

Road construction again made the trip to The Fork slower than Steve had anticipated. He called Vance to let him know he would be a bit late, twenty minutes maybe. Vance offered to order breakfast for Steve so it would be ready when he arrived; and Steve thanked him for doing that.

"But save room for dessert," Vance said. "Libby and Bobthecook have concocted a special kind of pie that has to be eaten here."

"Sounds mysterious, but I'm sure delicious as usual," Steve said, thanking Vance again.

While he drove – slowly due to construction traffic – Steve fielded a call from Harry. His senior salesperson was still struggling with the new compensation plan, the new focus on the more profitable software product, and with being asked to adapt to a new sales process – even if he had also been asked to contribute insights into what that process should include.

Harry vented. Steve listened. Traffic crawled.

Just as the construction zone ended and the highway expanded to its intended capacity, Harry grew silent, and Steve filled the void, speaking into the hands-free mic: "Harry, I understand that this is all new – it is for all of us – and I understand that change is not always comfortable. But the bottom line is that what worked for us once isn't working now and hasn't been working for a long time.

"I also appreciate your individualism and the pride you take in being your own man, in selling your own way. That spirit is admirable, and it will certainly be possible, even advantageous, for you to put your personal stamp on the sales process in real-world selling situations."

Harry tried to interject, but Steve pressed on. "Let me finish, Harry, because this is important, and it is absolutely essential that you get the point I'm about to make." Steve took a deep breath and exhaled slowly. He was nearing the diner. "Harry, we are at a critical juncture," he said, The Fork in sight and just ahead at the intersection. "We will only succeed, short-term and long-term, if we are all on the same page, all on the same team, and all using the same systems and processes. New and improved systems and processes."

He pulled into the parking lot, shifted into park and sat in the idling car.

"Hear me on this, now, okay? You have been a valuable contributor to our past success, Harry, but we need *present* success, and that will require new ways of working – together – for the greater good. Despite your accomplishments and contributions to the company, Harry, we need team players across the board. I'm confident you can continue to be successful utilizing the new strategy and processes we're implementing. But if you don't share that confidence, or if you choose to go your own way, well, I'm afraid *your own way* will have to be with another company. I hope it doesn't come to that, Harry. It certainly doesn't have to. But if your heart is not in this new mission, then you will be free to leave."

Moments of silence, but Steve could hear Harry breathing. Finally, a sigh, and then Harry said, "Okay, I get it. Still can't say I like it much, but I'll give it a chance and see what I can do with the new ways."

"Thank you, Harry. We can do this. We can *all* do this."

Steve took a moment to gather his thoughts, and then entered the diner. He waved to Vance and smiled at Libby. She was updating the daily pie board: *Tin Roof Pie*.

"Spin the tin, Jack," Libby called, and Jack put in motion the unique process of firing up the jukebox. After a few guitar chords, Steve recognized the song as *Tin Man* by the band America.

Steve approached the table, his breakfast platter and coffee already there but still steaming hot. He sat and shook hands with Vance.

"Just delivered," Vance said. "Your timing is perfect."

"Thank you again for ordering. Sorry to hold things up this morning."

"No worries. Couldn't be helped, I'm sure," Vance said. He nodded toward the jukebox, toward the song lyrics filling the air. "Very true, don't you think, that the tin man already had what he was asking for from The Wizard?"

Steve looked quizzically at Vance.

"Same for the Scarecrow and the Lion and for Dorothy, too, right? They already had the power to achieve their goals. All they had to do was look within, find what they needed, and then summon the brains and heart and courage and the *desire* to find their way."

"Okay," Steve said, "this is spooky. Have you been spying on me?"

Now Vance had the quizzical look.

"We just watched *The Wizard of Oz* for our family movie night. My daughter Abby picked it out."

Vance laughed. "Well, I can guarantee you that I haven't been spying on you, but maybe Libby has been. After all, she chose to make Tin Roof Pie this time."

Steve shook his head. "Just what is a Tin Roof Pie, anyway?"

"Glad you asked," Libby said, sidling up next to the table. "Perfect dessert after a hot breakfast. The crust is made with cereal flakes and peanut butter and corn syrup, all pressed into the pan, then filled with softened ice cream and topped with chopped peanuts. We let the whole thing freeze up pretty firm and then drizzle on chocolate syrup and whipped cream."

"Sounds a little *too* awesome," Steve said.

"Oh, it is," Libby affirmed. "Only trouble is you can't really transport it home if you have very far to drive."

"That *is* too bad," Steve said, "but I won't tell the family if you don't."

Libby laughed. "Anything else here, men?"

"We're good for now, I think," Vance said, looking to Steve for confirmation. Steve nodded and Libby disappeared into the kitchen.

Vance and Steve ate their breakfasts and chatted about their weeks. Steve shared more about the new family movie night tradition and about the lessons his kids took away from the land of Oz. He also shared that he had told his family how he appreciated the journey depicted in the movie and how it had made him think of his own journey, especially the path his business was now on.

"Funny how we can find parallels between what we are experiencing in day-to-day life and what we have chosen to focus on," Vance said. "You found a parallel between your journey and the quest of the main characters in the movie. Some would call it an epiphany or a coincidence, others might call it fate, still others would say it's the hand of God at work. Probably all the above. But it's also about being aware of influences and possibilities, and about where we direct our attention and *from* where we draw our lessons."

"I think you're right, Vance. Just like in the movie, it's all there for us to find if we only know where to look."

"Indeed it is, and the same is true for you and your situation, Steve. I'm no wizard," Vance said, "but I *am* an instrument in helping you find the path."

With the dishes cleared, they turned their discussion to Steve's progress since they were last together.

"So," Vance began, "how did it go last week?"

"Well, first," Steve began, "I think I should mention something that happened right before I got here this morning."

"Oh, what was that?"

"Harry called and was venting about not liking this and that. He was basically trying to derail things before we get them on track. I guess you could say he was trying to call my bluff."

"Except that it isn't a bluff, now, is it?"

"No sir," said Steve.

"So, he was venting. How far did you let that go, and how far did you take your response?" Vance asked.

Steve sat up straighter in the booth. "I think I handled it well. Very well, actually. I listened for a while, until it seemed he was losing steam. I figured that if Harry is ever going to get with the new program, he will at least need to know his objections have been heard."

"That sounds wise. What happened next?"

"Well, I told him I appreciated his spirit and his individualism and his past contributions. But I also told him – in no uncertain terms – that changes were needed from everyone, and that it was time we all worked from the same playbook if we were going to succeed. I also told him that if he couldn't go along and get along, he could always *move* along – not quite that bluntly, though."

"Oh boy," Vance said. "It sounds like you laid it on the line and were direct and assertive. In other words, you acted like the leader you are becoming. How did Harry take that?"

Steve smiled at the compliment, and then said, "He was quiet at first, and I simply allowed the silence. I could tell he was trying to process the information and the situation."

"And your tone, no doubt."

"Yes, that too, I suppose," Steve said. "But then Harry said a pretty remarkable thing."

Vance leaned in.

"Harry said he gets it even if he doesn't like it much yet. Still, he said he'd give this new way of doing things a chance and see how he can make it work."

"That sounds great," said Vance. "Did you believe him? Do you think he's being sincere or just telling you what you want to hear?"

"Well, Harry's a bit of a rebel, but I could detect a certain resignation in his voice. Not that he sounded beaten down exactly, but he sounded as if he could see that resistance was futile so he might as well give things a try."

"That's fantastic!" Vance said. "I think you've handled this tricky situation perfectly. My only advice going forward is that you find ways to continually affirm and praise Harry's *team* efforts. Do that with your entire team, too, of course, but it sounds like Harry's ego needs stroking more than Joe's and Sally's. He's used to doing things his way – right or wrong – and getting by with it. That means you're asking more of Harry than the others because you're really asking him to change his work personality and method of operation. Let him keep some of that bravado by affirming his positive efforts and building him up when you can."

"I'll definitely be sensitive to that," Steve said. "It will be a fine line to walk at times, I'm sure, but I see what you're getting at."

Libby came back by. "Took a fresh Tin Roof Pie out of the deep freeze a while back and put it in the refrigerated case to soften a bit. You fellas let me know when your bellies have room for some of that ridiculous deliciousness."

Steve laughed. "My belly may have room soon, but I'm seriously going to have to go up a belt size or let my pants out after all this pie. You don't happen to know a good alteration person, do you?"

Libby chuckled. "You know, I never thought of that. We could find someone and arrange a strategic partnership. Or at least just be generally in cahoots!" She stepped away, laughing heartily at the thought.

"Okay," Vance said, "so, it went well with Harry. How did the rest of your week go?"

"It all went pretty well, too," Steve said, "but while I was talking with our sales reps, I was surprised to learn that our overall sales process wasn't as detailed as I had thought. It is actually pretty 'loosey goosey' you might say. I was also surprised to learn that each person who is connected to the sales process had a different idea of how it actually flows."

"How so? How did you determine that?"

"Well, I asked our reps and our project engineers to join me; and I asked them to each bring their view of the sales process with them. But I also asked them not to confer with one another before we got together as a group."

"Smart of you to stipulate that," said Vance.

"I asked each person to share with me their first step in the process. Joe had his process start with a customer meeting, Sally started with a customer phone call, Harry with a proposal, and the project engineers were also different."

"Interesting. So, what did that tell you?"

"I guess it told me we each work independently with no common process. It confirmed my suspicions about that, actually."

"And how do you think that way of operating has been affecting your business so far?"

"I'm not sure," Steve hedged, "but I imagine it's not been in a positive way, hence my discussion with 'lone wolf' Harry."

Vance paused for a moment and then continued: "You mentioned proposals last week. Are your project engineers bothered when they take the time to scope a project, only to find out that the customer was never qualified? Are they upset, thinking they wasted their time putting together a project scope because a salesperson never bothered to ask the correct questions?"

"Yes," Steve said. "Unfortunately, that happens all the time. In fact, I'm always nervous that our project engineers are going to get so upset they'll leave. Aside from me, they're the only ones who can do that type of work. There constantly seems to be a rift between the salespeople and the project engineers. I'm sure it's damaging our culture."

Vance nodded. "I suspect you're right. So, what have you done about it so far?"

"Honestly, not much. I just help them work through the current issue and try to calm everyone down."

"But you really aren't addressing the core issue, are you?"

"No, I suppose not," Steve admitted. "I've been so busy trying to hang on to customers that I guess I just hoped the problem would go away."

Vance pursed his lips for a moment, and then said, "At least you acknowledge the seriousness of the problem and its danger to your future. But don't worry, Steve; I can help you fix the issue permanently."

"Well, that would be great, certainly. How do we do that?"

"Naturally, we keep working through this sales process. We can talk more about that, shortly. But first, what else did you learn when you went through the sales process exercise with your team?"

"I learned that even when we agreed on a certain sales process step, we still disagreed as to what should occur at each stage and what is needed to move to the next step in the process."

"That's not at all uncommon, Steve. What issues do you think that causes?"

"I guess the big one that occurs to me is that we aren't delivering consistency to our customers. That probably ripples through the entire customer experience, from initial contact to service after the sale – *if* we make the sale, that is."

Vance nodded. "I'm sure that's the case, and it's probably part of the reason you've had to spend so much time with customers; you are trying to fix issues that never should have come up in the first place."

"I bet you're right," Steve said. "I constantly hear complaints about issues that are oversights by my employees. I talk to them about it, of course, but now I understand it was my fault for never having a single unified, documented and detailed process that everyone follows."

"When you finally do have that unified process in place and it isn't being followed, the issue will be one of two things, in my view," Vance suggested. "One, someone didn't follow the process, so now you can hold them accountable. Or two, the process needs to be changed, because an employee is taking a different action to be more efficient or help the customer. Either way, the solution is simple."

"That makes total sense. But we'll definitely need that baseline."

"Exactly," Vance said. "The lack of a clear and consistent process also makes it very difficult to forecast future revenue. I know you haven't done that in the past, forecasting future revenue based on KPIs, I mean."

"KPIs?"

"Key Performance Indicators," Vance clarified. "Also called 'leading indicators' sometimes."

Steve nodded. "I've heard of those, but I guess I don't really understand what they are."

"Think of *leading* indicators as those actions that can indicate the probability of a future sale. On the other hand, a *lagging* indicator is an 'output' that has already taken place. You'll want to start with the results you want, via those lagging indicators and then work backward to identify the necessary actions – the leading indicators – to achieve those results. Now, you mentioned that you want to have $16M in revenue a year from now. Imagine if you ended the year at $15M, there would be nothing more you can do to find another $1M – the year is over. But, now, with leading indicators in play, we *can* do something about it. It is similar to knowing you are going to lose a game before the game is over. If you knew, through leading indicators, that you were on a path to be short of your goal you would change your actions to change your results. To make that possible, we'll need to identify those actions necessary to indicate we're on the right path to achieve, or exceed, $16M a year from now."

"I got it," said Steve. "I've been focused only on lagging indicators in the past."

"Now, let me be clear," Vance said. "Activities within each sales process step are essentially *miniature* leading indicators. If you identify what actions need to take place within each sales cycle step in order to move to the next step in the process, you create a predictive process for the closure of that sale. That's a leading indicator.

"Steve, I also asked you to consider the probabilities of closure at each sales cycle step, because that percentage will numerically indicate the likelihood of closing that particular deal. These probabilities of closure then help you forecast accurately, because they aren't based on each sales rep's opinion anymore; instead, they're based on the agreed-upon leading indicators of future success. We need to make our best estimate on the likelihood of closure at each sales cycle step now, but in a short period of time, you'll be able to base those probabilities of closure on the actual percentage that has taken place. It isn't a static event, either; it must constantly be adjusted to your past results."

"Sounds a little complex, but I'm sure I understand," said Steve. "You also mentioned that we'd talk today about CRMs. How does a CRM tie in?"

Libby topped off their coffee. "Ready for that pie yet?"

"Just about, "Vance said. "Wrapping up here in a few minutes."

"I'll get it to you straight away, then," she said.

As she stepped away, Vance returned to Steve's question. "First of all," he said, "CRM stands for Customer Relationship Management. You might have already heard of that. But here's how that connects: The reason we started with developing the sales process first is because your CRM is meant to be populated with some of the information you built into your new sales process. So, you need to devise the individual components of the sales process first so the CRM can track that information. Your CRM will help you accomplish the strategy and tactics you set forth, not the other way around."

"So, essentially if you don't develop your sales process first, it turns into a database of a lot of individual opinions?"

"I guess you could say that," Vance agreed. "You could enter information into your CRM, but without a process in place, it's just a digital version of your old process — or as it exists today, an individual process for each employee."

"Well, that wouldn't help us much, would it, considering our process itself is poorly defined?"

"No, it wouldn't, but now, with a well-defined sales strategy and sales process in place, you're ready to add your sales process to your CRM. In fact, your sales process *must* reside in a CRM."

"How do we get started toward building a good CRM?"

"You first need to determine what value or output you expect to receive from it," Vance said. "For next week, I'll want you to make a list of those important factors."

"Got it."

Vance reached into a folder, thumbed through some papers and finally produced a document detailing many key features of a CRM system, including scalability, training and support offered, cloud-based vs. software, and many more items. "This will get you started as you rank what is most important to your team. Of course, you can always call me if you have any questions."

Libby appeared, a plate of Tin Roof Pie in each hand. "Steve might not have any questions right now, but I do: Would you gentlemen prefer a fork or a spoon for your Tin Roof ice cream pie?"

CHAPTER TWENTY-ONE

The Best Treasure

On the way home, Steve fielded calls from Joe and Sally, too. They had questions and ideas, a couple of concerns, but mostly excitement about the potential of the new sales process being developed as well as the new compensation plan. Positive or negative, enthusiastic or hesitant, Steve was delighted to see his reps so engaged in the process. What once felt like a stagnant sales team culture was now alive and active.

Their questions and ideas raised others in Steve's mind. He took a nearby exit and stopped in a parking lot to jot down notes for the week ahead and for his next meeting with Vance. When he had finished recording his thoughts, Steve looked up through the windshield. He was parked in front of a vintage record store.

It called him inside.

Still sitting at the booth in the diner, Vance took a call, then stepped outside to continue the conversation. When he returned inside, Libby joined him.

"That was Nancy," he said. "She says she was going through some of Charlie's things. Said it became a bit of a treasure hunt, in fact, and that she came across something she thought I might like to have."

"Did she say what it was?" Libby asked.

"No, but she wants to bring it to the house soon, maybe next week."

Vintage was the operative word for the record store. There had to be thousands of old LPs and 45s. There were also some early CDs, cassettes and 8-tracks. Even a smattering of 78 RPM records and, amazingly, some old Edison phonograph cylinders. The place harkened back to Steve's childhood and teen years, and to memories of the music that once pervaded his parents' home.

Now, it also reminded him of The Fork and its eclectic music mix on the jukebox.

"Looking for anything in particular?" a middle-aged man asked. He was probably in his early 60s, Steve guessed. Bearded. Pony-tailed. Wearing wire framed glasses that kept sliding down his slender nose.

"Nothing in mind right now," Steve said. "Would love to look around a bit, though."

"Be my guest," the man said. "I always say the best treasure is the one you didn't even know you were looking for." With that he walked into a back room and left Steve to peruse the trove of long dormant musical memories. Realizing he could be there for hours on end, Steve concentrated his browsing to the section featuring popular music from the 1940s to the 1970s. Sorted by format and arranged alphabetically by decade and by artist within that decade, the history in the bins was mind boggling.

As he flipped through the albums, he discovered an old *Wizard of Oz* soundtrack on vinyl. He picked it out and set it aside, figuring the album cover would make for good wall art for Abby even if she would have no way of playing the record inside.

In the 45s section, dozens of Elvis Presley records lay at his fingertips. Among the obvious titles – *Jailhouse Rock, Love Me Tender, Suspicious Minds* and so on – he discovered a single of that more obscure Elvis tune he had heard played in the diner: *If I Can Dream.* He picked that one out, too – for himself.

The store had sheet music, too, dating from the 1880s at least, judging from his quick survey. Thumbing through the 1940s section, he came across sheet music for *Shoo-fly Pie and Apple Pan Dowdy* – Music by Guy Wood, Lyrics by Sammy Gallop. The cover art featured a cartoon of a hobo eyeing pies as they cooled in a windowsill, the hobo unaware that an aproned woman with a rolling pin stood behind him, ready to enforce the baker's justice. Perfect for Libby at The Fork, Steve thought, so he picked that one out, too.

Moments later, just about to abandon his search through the British Bands of the 70s and 80s LPs, he found yet another must-have – *Breakfast in America* by Supertramp. It reminded him not only of his breakfasts at The Fork, but also of the song playing when he had first entered the diner: *The Logical Song.*

Finally, having spent far more time in the record store than he had anticipated, at the checkout counter Steve noticed an array of yet-to-be inventoried 45s. One caught his eye: *The Doggie in the Window* by Patti Page.

In the car outside, he pulled out his cell phone and called Amy. "Hi," she answered. "What's up?"

With the Patti Page record in hand, Steve said, "Now, about that dog Abby wants…."

CHAPTER TWENTY-TWO
Light at the End of the Tunnel

Harry made a sale.

Even with the new sales process still not completely finalized and his view of the new sales compensation plan not entirely positive, Harry shared with Steve that he utilized the new approach to move a "stuck" prospect into the "sold" category. Better yet, he realized that the commission for this sale was more favorable than if it would have been for supporting an existing client.

Surprisingly, it seemed Harry was becoming a convert, and Steve couldn't wait to tell Vance. Except that Vance had not yet arrived when Steve entered the diner.

"He's not here quite yet," Libby said. She came around the counter and hugged Steve. "Feel free to take your place in the booth and I'll bring you a 'cuppa joe'."

"Actually, before I do that, I have something for you," Steve said. "He reached into his notebook and pulled free the sheet music for *Shoo-fly Pie and Apple Pan Dowdy.*

"Oh, my goodness, will you look at that!" Libby placed the sheet music on the counter and hugged Steve again. "Very thoughtful of you, ol' buddy. I think I'll frame it and put it up over by the jukebox. Next time I make the Shoofly, I'll easel-it-up here on the counter." She picked up the sheet music again and viewed it at arms' length. "Ah, that sure is perfect, Steve. I'm grateful to you."

"Well, I'm grateful to you as well," Steve said. "It's not just Vance helping me out; it's also you and Bobthecook and Jack and Jenny and everyone here – in fact, it's the diner itself, too – helping me see the world in a different light."

"That sure makes me happy to hear that," Libby said. She was beaming even more than usual. "So, tell me, friend, how is your work going? Are you making progress with Vance's help?"

"Oh, absolutely," Steve said. "He's opened my eyes and given me so many ideas and tools to use, it's been amazing. When Vance advises me to try something, it seems maddeningly obvious at times, and yet I would never have seen these solutions on my own. Because of him, we're trying new alternatives and putting things together in ways we never could have imagined before."

"That makes me happy, too," Libby said. "And speaking of putting things together in new ways … Jack, fire up the box and put the lime in the coconut!"

In moments, from inside the jukebox, Harry Nilsson sprang to life with the novelty song *Coconut*.

"Haven't heard that one in a very long time," Steve said.

Just then the cowbell sounded, and Vance walked in. "Ah, must be Lime in the Coconut Pie day at The Fork, eh?"

"You got it, mister," Libby said. "And look what Steve brought me. Won't that be perfect to display next time we do the Shoofly Pie?"

Vance smiled broadly. "Perfect, indeed. Very thoughtful gesture, Steve." He motioned to the booth. "Shall we?"

Once seated, Vance looked at Steve. "May I offer an observation?" he asked.

"Of course."

"You truly do seem like a changed man from the first time you came into this diner. Back then you were really down, and, if I may say so, downright miserable. Now you're, well, you certainly seem happy and optimistic. And kind. You seem to have adopted an attitude of gratitude and generosity."

"Thank you, Vance. If that's true – and I guess it is – I owe it all to you."

"Oh, no, you don't. I may have fanned a flame here and there, but if I may revisit our discussion from last time, you always had the brains and the heart and the courage – and that deep-down desire – to realize your potential. And to help your company do the same."

"I suppose," Steve said. "But what you fanned has gone from flame to fire to inferno. I am, no, *we* are as a company, on fire to turn things around. And the really great news I've been dying to share with you, is that we're already doing it!"

Vance cocked his head slightly and squinted. "What do you mean? What's happened?"

Steve's smile was spreading and stayed in full bloom as he spoke. "Well, as you know, we haven't quite finalized the sales process yet, nor have we implemented a CRM. In fact, we've got a ton of work ahead of us; I know that. And yet, just the fact that we are attacking this thing as a team is already paying dividends."

"How so?"

"I first saw the changes in attitude," Steve began. "Sally and Joe are more optimistic and energized than ever. And Harry has gone from complete resistance to reluctant participant and now to full-on cheerleader!"

"Really? *Harry?*" Vance looked skeptical.

"You bet," Steve said. "In fact, he's the first to make a sale in our ever-evolving sales process. His somewhat grudging openness to trying new ways has already borne fruit. And suddenly, he gets it. He sees the potential that lies ahead!"

Vance rocked back in the booth. "Well, Steve, I am a bit flabbergasted. I've seen quick turnarounds before, but it usually requires actually completing the refinement of the sales process and the full implementation of the CRM. Nonetheless, I think this shows the importance and influence of the right attitude as an intangible in the bigger equation." He offered his hand to Steve and they shook. "Congratulations on expertly guiding your team to a place of belief in future possibilities. That's an enormous accomplishment."

For a while, Steve was too giddy to talk nuts-and-bolts business, so the two men ordered and ate and rode the wave of Steve's euphoria. But only to a point. Eventually, Vance cautioned Steve, saying, "I'm excited that *you're* excited, Steve, but I should warn you that it's not always going to be smooth sailing from here on out. Take a moment, as you are, to celebrate this first success, but don't lose sight of the fact that there's much hard work still to be done."

Steve nodded in agreement, but the smile remained.

"So, with that thought in mind," Vance said, "let's get down to business, shall we? Where are you with your sales process?"

"We're nearly there," Steve said. "Some fine-tuning left, of course, but we're pretty much all on the same page now, and I think that's what gave Harry the proper direction to land that new customer."

"Excellent! I'll leave that in your capable hands, then. And how did it go last week with your thoughts and discussions on a CRM?"

"That went well, too. We were generally in agreement."

"And what did you come up with?"

Steve opened his folder and retrieved his notes. "I brought back the document you provided and here's what we believe we need." He handed the papers to Vance.

Vance took a few moments to read the notes. Finally, he said, "I notice that training and support, a web-based application, and email integration were rated with the highest importance. On the other hand, integration with other applications – such as quote management, marketing, and social media – were rated low, along with, let's see..." Vance scanned the page. "Ah, yes, custom reporting was rated low also, while document storage and pipeline review were in the middle."

"Yes, that's right," Steve said.

"All in all, I think you and your team have done a sensible job of prioritizing the areas that are most important."

"Thanks. It was kind of difficult because we've never actually used our CRM, but we did a little research to understand the full range of capabilities across the spectrum of our CRM and other available systems. After doing that, the task wasn't too bad."

Libby came by, topped off their coffee and cleared away the dishes. Vance knew that Steve had already invested in a CRM, but he wasn't sure that what Steve had purchased would fulfill all of his company's needs.

So, Vance educated Steve about some CRM system vendors he often recommends. He was pleased that Steve took plenty of notes.

"Steve, I'd like you to take all this under consideration, do your own research and then make a selection for next time."

Steve exhaled heavily. He looked concerned. "What's wrong?" Vance asked.

"Oh, I guess I'm just projecting the week ahead and trying to figure out how I can do this selection process justice. It sure seems like this is a critical decision to be made and I don't want to rush it. I sure wish I had your background in this and your experience with all these vendors."

"Okay, I understand that. It can certainly be overwhelming, and you've been a real trouper so far." He took a pen and, reading upside down, circled three vendor names on Steve's page of notes. "I'm very confident, based on what I know about your business, your industry, your markets and your team, that these are the three you would eventually settle on as your finalists. Might as well start there, I suppose."

"Great! Thanks, Vance, I really appreciate that."

The men narrowed their discussion to the three vendors, with Vance offering information about each CRM product. They discussed the pros and cons of each system and compared and contrasted some fundamental features and benefits.

"Thank you," Steve said. "I'll get on this right away."

"Now, regardless of which system you choose, we need to talk about how to get the most from your CRM."

"Okay. Sounds like that might also provide some key information to help us determine the selection criteria."

"Absolutely," Vance said. "Now, first of all, it's important to have your sales team involved when selecting the CRM that will be used. You need to include the people who will be using it. There's no denying that features are important, but if your CRM isn't salesperson-friendly, you won't get the buy-in you need for its usefulness to be realized. Were your reps involved in your original CRM selection?"

"No, I selected our CRM based on what a friend had recently chosen for his company. His business is really different from ours, and I believe his needs are as well," Steve said.

"I understand," Vance said. "It isn't uncommon for business owners not to include their sales team in the decision, as well as to consider their unique needs first."

Steve paused before responding. "Although I don't like the idea of spending all that money on our original CRM and then not ever using it, I do recognize the need to get it right this time – not only in selection, but its usage too."

"That's great, Steve. Now, if it's difficult to include all three of your reps, include at least one from your team. If you were to pick one of the salespeople who is more of a leader the team will often listen to and follow, who would that be?"

"I suppose that would be Joe. Sally looks up to him, and although Harry is kind of a lone ranger, he respects Joe and his experience."

"Great, consider including all three or just Joe. If you include just Joe, and he agrees with the CRM selected, then the other two will be more inclined to follow."

"Got it," Steve said. "That makes sense to me."

Vance sipped his coffee and looked over his notes. "Now, you mentioned Training and Development as an important feature. While most CRMs provide written documentation, videos, and other self-paced training, consider what's important to your organizational needs. Plan for gaps. In many cases, the available training materials will not cover every CRM feature the organization plans to use. Identify any gaps and plan for how these may be filled, whether internally or via an external consultant. Also, consider who might be your internal expert. This person would be the go-to resource for questions and could provide additional training as needed. You will also need to document all processes and tips gathered from training to facilitate future education of other staff members."

"Actually, there is someone on Carl's staff that would be perfect in that role."

"And Carl is your Product Engineer – do I remember that correctly?"

"Right you are."

"Okay, that sounds appropriate," Vance said. "Consider what type of 'train-the- trainer' content that person will need."

"Got it."

"Great," Vance said. "Now, what other departments would need to gain access to your CRM?"

"I'm not sure," Steve admitted. "I tend to think of that only in terms of my sales team. Who else might normally be included?"

"Well, that could be anyone else who would be involved in the sales process or anyone who interacts directly with your customers."

"Okay, "Steve said, "obviously that would include the sales team, marketing and project engineers. Our customer service department would also be involved with project or account management; I didn't initially think of them."

"Good. Just make sure you consider anyone else that would fit that description. You want to ensure that your entire organization uses the CRM to document customer interactions so that any single employee can see where a customer is in the process at any given time. Allowing each department that interacts with customers access to the CRM ensures that everyone more effectively manages their customer relationships and sees the big picture at any point in time."

"Makes sense to me," Steve said. "I never would have thought of it that way."

Vance continued: "You'll want to gather the key information you already have, of course, so it can be uploaded to your CRM. This will give you a quick start and your team won't have to add every detail about every current customer into the CRM. After this quick start data is entered, however, you'll need to enter other key data you have that you anticipate needing to access in the future."

"Again, that makes sense," Steve said. "And the person I have in mind on Carl's team should be able to help us do that."

"Excellent. Now, you're also going to want to customize your CRM to fit your language and processes. After going through your selection process and then training, the last thing you want to happen is to have your sales team not like the CRM you selected because they don't understand what the terms or language means within the software. The key is to customize the software to incorporate your internal language and processes. This includes sales cycle steps, lead sources, reports, dashboards, and much more."

"Got it."

"Next, and perhaps most important," Vance said, "is that you'll want to establish expectations for your team."

"I'm not sure I know what you mean, Vance. What kinds of expectations?"

Vance gave a quick smile. "Are you familiar with the term 'carrot and stick'?"

"Yes, I think so."

"Well, with each new CRM implementation, user adoption requires a 'carrot and stick' approach. The 'carrot' is how you entice users to *want* to use the CRM and the 'stick' is what you *require* those CRM users to do. The 'carrot' means you'll have to explain the CRM's value to the user, not the value received by management. Now, of course, the CRM will make it easier for you to analyze your company's performance, track selling trends, and assess your sales team's productive health, but ultimately, your sales team doesn't care about that; they care about why using a CRM is better for *them*."

"So, why *is* it better for them? What do they gain from it given all the effort they will have to put into it?"

"Many reasons," Vance began, "but here are a few. First, it can help them understand what they'll earn faster. They can see their pipeline grow and know when deals will close; therefore, they know how much they'll make – no more surprises! It's also a centralized place to track prospect interaction. It'll make it easier for them to find when they last talked to a prospect, remember what they promised to do and by when; and they can also find information about proposals, contracts, etc., that have been stored under a prospect's name or their company."

"That's a lot right there," Steve said.

"There's much more, of course. They can also store all their notes about prospects in one place. Steve, have you ever had a call with a prospect or client, and they start talking about something that you don't remember off-hand? Kind of throws you off – makes it hard to get your bearings. Ever experience that?"

"Unfortunately, quite a few times," Steve said. He lifted his cup and sipped coffee.

"Well, imagine being able to type their name into your computer or into your phone during that call and having all their information in one place."

"That would be nice. It would avoid some of those embarrassing situations from happening again."

"Exactly," Vance said. He continued: "Now, on to the 'stick.' There's an old saying that goes like this: 'If it's not in the CRM, it doesn't exist.' So, whether it's a client conversation or a proposal that was sent, set the expectation that you won't have a conversation or pay commission to any salesperson unless the information is entered in the CRM."

"I see. I'll need to be firm and disciplined about that."

"Absolutely. You'll also need to make sure that you set the example by using it as described, as well as checking the CRM before asking questions of your reps. What message do you think you would send if you ask Sally about how her meeting went on Monday, when she already had entered all that information in the CRM?"

"I suppose at the most basic level it would tell her I didn't look inside the CRM. Beyond that, it would probably send the message that I'm not committed to it or don't see the value in it myself."

"And what future actions would she take, given that you don't look in the CRM often?"

Steve sighed. "She would probably stop adding her information into the CRM."

"That's correct. And you might think she caused the problem, but in reality, it was *your* actions that caused the issue. This is especially important in client meetings; review their pipeline of deals carefully before sitting down with them. It will make your meetings more efficient, but it will also tell them that you are reviewing the CRM and that you are committed to it. It's also important to comment on their pipeline in the middle of the week, so they don't just add in the information the day before you meet."

"I see," Steve said, jotting down a note. "Otherwise, I would be running reports to see our progress, and it would only be current on the day I meet with them."

"Exactly!" Vance rocked back in the booth. "Hey, you're starting to sound like a real sales manager!"

Steve laughed and felt his cheeks redden a bit.

"Okay, Steve, lastly, I want you to consider integrating your email into your CRM. I know you didn't think that integrating your CRM with other systems was important, at least not now, but integrating your CRM and email will make it much easier for your company in the long run. You can integrate them so once you type the client or prospect's name, it will link that email to their CRM record. In the end, anything you can do to make it easier and more powerful for your team will increase the chances of full adoption."

"I didn't realize there were so many areas to consider," Steve said, "but I can see why if you don't do all that you described, we'll have spent money on a CRM that nobody uses and we can't retrieve the necessary data when we want it and need it."

"That's very true."

Steve cleared his throat and sat up straighter. "So, Vance, it feels like you've given me everything I need to be successful. I just mix the lime with the coconut and mix 'em both up, right?" The song was playing again in the background; someone had just ordered a slice of the day's special pie.

Vance laughed. "Except that there are a lot of limes and a ton of coconuts to throw into the mix."

"Point taken," Steve said. "Is that all I need?"

"Well, it's very good start, but we haven't yet discussed sales leadership. So far, we've focused on building the sales infrastructure you need, but that is like building a shiny and potentially fast new race car. Next, we'll need to focus on who does the driving and how it is driven to get the most out of the vehicle."

"Sounds like another intriguing element I haven't thought much about, I guess," Steve admitted.

"We'll talk about that next time," Vance said. "For now, focus on identifying your future CRM and start putting into place the actions we discussed that will be necessary to get the most out of it."

"Wow!" Steve exclaimed. "I had no idea there were so many critical elements to consider and implement. I have a lot of work in front of me, but I'm beginning to see the light at the end of the tunnel." He chuckled. "At least now it doesn't feel like the light of an oncoming train!"

CHAPTER TWENTY-THREE

A Man's Reach

Lately, Steve found himself drawn to people and places as he had never been before. On his drive back to the office from The Fork, he again saw the exit where the fast food restaurant beckoned. He wasn't thirsty and wasn't hungry, of course. He was only curious. Curious about the cashier and about the woman with the children. Curious about whether his acts of paying it forward had made even a small difference in their lives.

He was tempted to take the exit. So tempted that he clicked on his turn signal and slowed down. But just as quickly, Steve changed his mind. Some things are better left unknown, he figured, better left in the realm of faith. And why did he crave knowing what happened anyway? Would knowing make the lives of those young women better? No, it would only satisfy his own pride, and he figured that was a foolish and unnecessary thing. Better to give the gift and move on. To be satisfied with the gesture alone.

As he drove past the exit, the "starfish story" came to mind. He knew there were different versions of the parable, but in the one he recalled, an old man was walking along a beach littered with thousands of starfish who had been washed ashore by a storm. He came upon a boy who was gathering up the starfish, one by one, and returning them to the ocean. The man challenged the boy, telling him there were too many starfish and that he couldn't possibly make a difference. At that, the boy picked up another starfish and sent it back into the waves, saying, "I made a difference to that one."

Steve smiled at the lesson from that parable. It was the kind of story that Vance might share to make a point, but Steve had recalled it on his own. It pleased him to know that he had moved on from a place of desperate hopelessness to mindful selflessness.

Late that afternoon, the doorbell rang at Vance's home. Sometimes his wife forgot her key, but it was a bit too early for her to be home. He rose from his desk chair, walked into the Living Room, and opened the door.

It was Nancy.

"I hope I'm not interrupting you, Vance," she said, stepping inside. "I know how busy you must be these days."

"Of course not," Vance said. "Never too busy to spend time with one of my favorite people. Come. Sit down. Let's visit."

Nancy took a seat on the sofa while Vance sat in a high-backed chair, facing her, a magazine-strewn coffee table between them.

"Where are my manners?" Vance said, rising again. "Can I get you something? Coffee? A soda? Some water or lemonade?"

"Oh, no, but thank you, Vance. I really can't stay long. Off to visit the grandkids for a couple days. I knew I'd be driving by, so I thought I'd stop in for just a bit. Still, I should have called…"

"Nonsense," Vance assured her. "Stop in anytime." He sat again and leaned forward. "Tell me, Nancy, how are you doing these days? I think of you more often than you can imagine."

She looked down for a moment. "I'm doing okay," Nancy said, and then looked up at Vance again. "Thank you for your recent visit and then for your phone call a couple weeks back. It made my day. I've been so blessed to have people Charlie worked with and cared about checking in on me. It truly helps to know I'm in their thoughts and prayers."

"Of course. So, the grandkids have been keeping you busy, you say?"

"Oh, sure. They were Charlie's pride and joy. Mine, too. Again, a blessing."

"I'm certain of that."

"And your daughter in Florida, how is she getting along after the hurricane?" Nancy asked.

"Doing great," Vance said. "She'll visit us here at home soon. She weathered the storm well."

At that, Nancy pulled a bag onto her lap. Vance had been so surprised and pleased to find Nancy at his door that he hadn't even noticed she had brought her purse and another bag inside with her. "Weathering the storm reminds me that I have something for you," she said.

"Now, Nancy, you certainly didn't need to—"

"It's from Charlie, actually. I've been going through his things bit by bit and came across something he intended for you. Something he just never got around to, well, to giving you."

"He was the most thoughtful man I think I've ever known," Vance said warmly. "Just knowing him was the greatest gift."

"Thank you, Vance. He felt the same about you. Very much so." She reached into the bag and pulled out a small sculpture. She handed it to Vance across the coffee table.

He took the sculpture into both hands, held it there in his palms, and studied it. Made of twisted wire – hundreds of twisted wires, in fact, it was a small tree, its branches outstretched as if blown by strong winds.

"Charlie left a note in the bag with it. He had jotted down some thoughts, kind of random, but I think we can guess what he intended." Nancy retrieved her reading glasses from her purse and held the note up before her eyes. "For Vance. Weather the storms. Bend but stay strong. Remember that a man's reach should exceed his grasp."

She removed her glasses, looked at Vance, and handed him the note.

Vance shook his head gently from side to side. His eyes were glistening. "Good reminders, certainly," he said. "And that last part is a from a Robert Browning poem, if I recall correctly."

Nancy reached into bag again. She pulled out another tree sculpture, identical to the first, and placed it on the coffee table. "I'd like you to have this one, too," she said. "It was very common for Charlie to buy two of something, one to keep and one to give away. I think he'd like for you to have both of these and do the same."

"Yes, that sounds very much like Charlie," Vance said. "But don't you want to hang on to this one, Nancy? Seems like it would be a nice reminder of Charlie in your home."

Nancy shook her head. "I think he'd rather you have it. I have so many wonderful memories of Charlie and our life together. But frankly, I know I need to start paring down some possessions. Charlie wouldn't want me to be alone in that big house. He told me that once. Worried that it would be like living in a museum." She smiled. "He was right, of course."

Vance read the note again. He looked at the wire tree sculpture in his hand and the one on the table. He nodded. "Thank you, Nancy. I know just who Charlie would want me to give it to."

The doorbell rang. "Excuse me for just a moment, will you, Nancy?"

"Of course, but actually I do need to get going." She rose with him and they walked to the door.

Vance opened the door and found his wife fumbling inside her purse. "Looks like I forgot my key again," she said. Looking up then, she saw Nancy and beamed at the sight of her old friend. She stepped inside and the women hugged for a long time.

When they separated, Nancy said, "Hello, Elizabeth. So good to see you again. Sorry I can't stay and visit longer."

CHAPTER TWENTY-FOUR

Nothing Is Impossible If You Dare to Dream

Steve found himself running late again, not because of road construction, but because Abby's new puppy had made off with one of his shoes. By the time he found it (complete with random teeth marks adding new character to the patterned leather) and gathered up his things, he was ten minutes behind schedule. He knew Vance wouldn't mind, but once he was in his car, he called Vance at home.

"No worries at all," Vance said. "A puppy ate my homework a few times, so I completely understand."

Steve laughed. "It's certainly a new experience and a new dynamic around here. It seems the smaller they are, the more they run our lives. I used to be aware of that with our kids, but now this puppy has taken over the household and is forcing us to alter our routines."

"Change is difficult and stressful, Steve. I've been impressed with how well you've been weathering the storms during this process." Vance looked at the wire tree sculpture now on his desk. "So, I'm certain you can adapt and find order in this brave new world of puppy-driven chaos, too."

"I'm sure I will," Steve said. "Thanks for understanding. I'll see you at the diner shortly."

In fact, Steve made it to The Fork just as Vance pulled in. Inside, Vance stopped and inhaled deeply. "Ah," he said, "I never get tired of smelling that potpourri of coffee, bacon and pie."

"It's certainly intoxicating," Steve agreed. "Enough to keep bringing a person back." Libby rushed by, hugged them both and scurried behind the counter. "What's the pie du jour?" Steve asked.

Gathering up glasses of orange juice for a couple of patrons seated near the door, Libby nudged the daily pie sign with her elbow. "Almost couldn't fit the name of this one on the sign," she laughed.

Steve leaned in closer to read the smaller print: *Nothing Is Impossible If You Dare to Dream Pie*

"And what's the song for this one, I wonder," Vance said. "Hey, Jack, what are you spinning today?"

Without speaking, Jack tapped and kicked the machine until the strains and rising refrains of *The Impossible Dream* began softly and soon crescendoed.

"Thanks, Jack," Vance shouted over the music as he and Steve made their way to the corner booth.

"I've heard this song before, but way back," Steve said. "Who sings it?"

"Andy Williams did this version, if memory serves. But I know it's been covered by a multitude of crooners over the years." Vance had emphasized the word "crooners." He continued: "I'm older than you, Steve, so my memory probably goes a bit further back, but I believe this was from the mid-1960s. It was in the midst of the civil rights era, just before Vietnam and not long before that fateful year, 1968, when we lost Dr. Martin Luther King and Bobby Kennedy. This song was popular at the dawn of the protest era; and as I recall, it came from the musical, *Man of La Mancha*."

"Isn't that the one about Don Quixote?"

"The same."

Steve shook his head, "But wasn't Don Quixote crazy? I mean, didn't he fight windmills or something?"

"He 'tilted' at windmills, yes," said Vance. "And I know where you are going. You're thinking that if Quixote was insane, why should we take seriously his quest – and by the way, *The Quest* was the name of the song in the musical, I believe? In other words, why should we find inspiration in the anthem of a crazy man?"

"Yeah, that's pretty much what I was wondering," Steve confirmed.

Vance sighed and looked wistfully out the window. "Well, it seems to me that most quests that are worthwhile seem a little crazy at first, and certainly insurmountable at times. In fact, envisioning a crazy quest – that is, to see possibilities no one else can see – can be a daunting task. I think it's that fear of something new and untamed that keeps so many people from pursuing their dreams. Entrepreneurship is exactly that – leaving your old corporate life behind and taking a risk."

When Vance turned back to Steve, he could see that Steve was forming new questions. "So, is it a noble thing," Steve asked, "to pursue an impossible dream? Is it courageous? Or just foolish?"

Vance smiled. "Perhaps all of the above. But who's to say what's impossible unless you try? Look at your business, for example; you made the possible out of something *impossible.*"

A grin suddenly appeared on Steve's face. "I guess I never looked at it that way."

"Wait till you try our *Nothing Is Impossible If You Dare to Dream Pie,*" Libby gushed. "It's a coconut custard pie that makes its own crust. It's so easy, I might just have to add it to the regular menu."

"*Another* coconut pie?" Vance asked.

"You can never have too much coconut," Libby said. "Besides," she whispered, "we bought too much last time when we concocted the lime and coconut pie."

Steve laughed; and after Libby filled their cups and took their orders, the men got down to business.

"So, have you settled on a CRM yet?" Vance began.

"Yes, we have," Steve said. He revealed the chosen system to Vance, who gave it a thumbs-up sign. "And I did as you suggested," Steve continued, "and involved Joe. He brought some really good perspective."

"Was he pleased you invited him to be part of the process?"

"Yes, and I think a bit shocked. I usually just do all the work and he was very excited to be asked. Sally and Harry were pleased that Joe was involved too – although I think Harry was also relieved that I didn't ask *him* to be involved. Both of them shared information with Joe to bring to the table."

125

As if taking her cue, Libby brought a small plate with two spoons and set it down on the corner booth table. Each spoon held a dollop of the coconut custard pie."

"You weren't kidding," Steve said. "That is outstanding. Another winner!" Vance's smile confirmed Steve's verdict.

"I'll save you a whole one," Libby said to Steve before stepping away.

Vance dabbed at the corners of his mouth and sipped his coffee. Then he said, "I'm glad you involved Joe and that the others supported this. I assume that took some of the burden off of you as well?"

"Yes, it did. I guess I don't need to do everything myself after all. Maybe I'm not as indispensable as I thought I was."

"I wouldn't quite go that far," Vance said, "but as long as you have the right people and the right processes in place, your company should be able to operate without you being involved *all* the time."

"It's funny," Steve said. "I guess I thought I had to be involved or things wouldn't get done. This is part of the reason that I've been so exhausted all the time, and also why I was gone from home so often."

"I know, Steve, but I wanted you to come to that realization on your own, rather than having me tell you."

Steve smiled. "I suppose I *am* more accepting of information when it is my idea!"

Vance tapped his coffee mug against Steve's. "Cheers to that! Actually, it's that way for everyone. Which, by the way, is the perfect transition to today's topic – sales management. But before we get to that, I want to find out what you really love to do."

"What I love to do? Not sure I follow, Vance."

"I want you to think back into your past about a job, or a period of time, or even a single day, where you went home thinking 'now, *that* was a great day!' Take a minute and think about that."

Steve picked up his coffee cup, raised it near his lips, but hesitated. He gazed into the black pool and seemed to get lost in thought there. He closed his eyes for a few seconds, and then opened them and finally said, "Wow, that's more difficult than it should be. Surely, I should be able to think of at least one day that was great. I mean, I've had great days with my family of course, but I have a feeling that's not what you're asking."

"That's true," Vance said. "I want you to dig deep and find something that gave you a sense of fulfillment and purpose, a sense of joy, a sense of excitement. The kind of thing where if you didn't have to eat and sleep you could have kept going for days on end. Does that help put the question in perspective?"

"I think so," Steve said. "Not sure it makes it easier, but I understand better what you are looking for."

"Take your time. In fact, let's eat while you think about it," Vance said, noticing Libby heading their way with their breakfasts.

So they did. For Steve it was a little uncomfortable at first; their meals had always included a side dish of conversation. But he did as Vance asked and lost himself in thought as he ate.

As they finished their breakfasts, Vance noticed a sudden smile on Steve's face. "Well?" he asked.

Steve put down his fork. "I guess I'd have to go back to around the time I started the company, maybe that first year or so. We were growing so fast in those days that every day was exciting. We were building our new software, constantly making changes to improve it and how we marketed it to our customers. Most of all, we were working as a team."

"That's good, Steve. Go on."

"You know, the more I think about it, I guess what I liked most was developing and refining the software. I really enjoyed the constant exploration of how we could improve it. Those kinds of changes haven't really happened lately; that kind of *energy* has been missing for a while now. Maybe that's why we're having trouble competing."

"I think you're onto something there," Vance said. "And I can relate to what you're saying. It wasn't easy for me to answer that question when Charlie asked it of me, either. In fact, I had to go back eight years to zero in on just one part of a single day, that's all, just one fleeting portion of a day that made me feel fully alive, like I was doing what I'd been put on this earth to do."

Steve was listening intently, so Vance continued, saying, "I realized I had worked my way up the corporate ladder, and then, when I got there, I didn't love what I was doing anymore. I was in a series of meetings every day, and most days half the meetings didn't really even need to take place. The company was so large that they couldn't make common sense decisions quickly; they thought they needed to meet about a single topic for months when the decision was obvious. To me, at least.

"I didn't feel listened to anymore. Now, don't get me wrong," Vance said, "I didn't expect my boss, the CEO, to do what I wanted every time; but

I felt as if I had lost my voice, and that decisions were being made about my department without me being listened to. Bureaucracy was rampant and corporate politics were more important than getting the job done. I was spending all my time with peers and senior leadership and I was no longer working with my team.

"You see, that's what Charlie was after, too. He made me realize that I missed the coaching, the mentoring, the teaching – all that was gone for me. It wasn't until I made the decision to 'go out into the field' that I felt alive again. I was working with my salespeople and sales managers and was using my wisdom to help them – and they really appreciated it. At first, they were nervous about me coming out into the field, but they found I could provide real value.

"I wanted to do more of it, of course, but my boss thought me going out into the field was a waste of time. But, don't you see, Steve, that type of work is what I *craved*, it was what I needed to feel alive again; and Charlie helped me realize that."

"The rest is history, right?" Steve interjected. "Is that what led you here?"

"Absolutely. When I finally allowed myself to see what I was passionate about, it also showed me where my real value lay. It wasn't long after that, then, that I transitioned into what I do now, where I can teach and mentor and make a real difference in peoples' lives again. I feel alive, Steve! I love what I do! And I want that same thing for you."

Vance waited a few more moments for Steve to respond. He didn't want to rush the realization – the epiphany – he could see forming in Steve's eyes.

"Hearing you talk about your need to get back closer to the field operations, Vance, makes me realize something. I think I've been thrust into the role of a business owner and CEO and all that brings with it. But what I really love to do is to work on developing and refining software. Unfortunately, I haven't been able to do that for a long time. To keep the company functioning, I've turned into an executive, an administrator, and mostly into a salesperson, someone trying to save my company's customers. I really don't think I am that good at it and I really don't like doing it."

"Then why have you been doing that work, Steve?"

Steve shook his head slowly, a look of resignation crossing his face. "I've been doing this work because I haven't felt my sales team was capable."

Vance's broad smile belied Steve's sudden sadness.

"I'm glad you can smile about it, Vance," he said.

"Okay, I know, it's not a joyous revelation at first," Vance said. "But it should be soon enough. You see, Steve, I'm thrilled to see you come to that realization. It's a pivot point between where you've been – and what has made you struggle so – and where you need to go. Don't get me wrong, I think it's essential for a business owner to spend time with customers and his sales team at times; but to do that exclusively and to ignore what truly makes you happy – well, that's a recipe for disaster.

"So, tell me," Vance continued, "how would you carve out such a role for yourself?"

"I don't see how I can, Vance. I don't think I can do exactly what I want and still keep up with all my other responsibilities."

Vance pushed his coffee cup aside and leaned in closer to Steve. "Put those other responsibilities on hold for a moment. Concentrate on what *you* want to do and what would bring the company the most value given your true skill set."

Steve looked down at the familiar tabletop pattern; a few moments later, he peered out the window for a bit. Finally, he said he wanted to focus more on the technical side of the business, that he wanted to work more with the project engineers and software developers. "My whole career has been doing that; I was just kind of thrust into the role of sales and marketing leader and CEO when I started my own company."

"I understand," Vance said. "That has happened to many other CEOs as well."

Libby topped off their coffees but did not interrupt the obviously intense meeting.

"Let's shift gears a bit," Vance continued. "Tell me what you do today with regard to managing your sales team. How do you engage with them on typical basis?"

"Well, as you know, I've been out of the office a lot, so most of our interaction is by phone or email. They ask me a lot of questions about current customers and sometimes about new opportunities. Most of the time I just respond to their questions."

"You don't sit down with them on a regular basis and review their sales pipeline or all their current opportunities, is that correct?"

Steve looked down at the tabletop again. "No. I just haven't had time."

"But could it also be because you don't enjoy doing that?"

"That's probably true," Steve admitted. I used to meet with them more often in the past, but these days when it happens, I think it's because I feel obligated to."

"And that's why I asked you what you loved to do and what you are best at, Steve. Those activities are typically sustainable because you *want* to do them. It's hard – if not impossible – to sustain an activity we don't like to do; we find reasons to avoid it."

"I'm sure that's true for me," Steve said.

"But you see, sales leaders need to sit down face-to-face weekly with each of their sales reps, reviewing their sales pipeline, coaching them through opportunities, removing obstacles in their path, co-traveling with them, and when necessary, holding them accountable to their required activities and goals. Hear me now, Steve, for this is critical: *Sales leaders love to do those things, but they don't like to develop software!*"

Steve looked dejected again. "I guess in some ways we're opposites, huh?"

"Behaviorally, yes," Vance agreed. "But don't lose sight of this: we need all kinds of different people to make a company work, but for each individual and for the company to succeed, we need each person to do what they do best."

Steve sat up straighter. "I don't mind going on a sales call with a rep to try to convert a highly-developed prospect," he said. "It's the nurturing of *new* prospects I don't like very much."

"Understandable," Vance said. "And my guess is you like playing the role of the visionary and the product development expert. Is that correct?"

"Yes, it is. How'd you know?"

Vance smiled. "Oh, I've done this a few times, Steve."

"I'm sure you have."

"Okay, so this is what I would like you to do for our next meeting. Keep track of your activities this week and write down, at a high level, what you're doing and put those activities in one column. Then, next to that column, create two more columns, one for what you *like* to do and the other for what you are good at. If you are doing an activity you don't like and aren't good at, don't put check marks in the second and third columns. Each activity can have zero, one or two checkmarks – it's purely up to you."

"Okay."

"And when we get together next time, Steve, we'll talk about what you put together and devise a plan to get you doing more of what you like to do and are good at. Ultimately, my friend, I'm confident that those are the things that will help your company grow!"

Steve smiled, but only halfway.

"Chin up," Vance said. "Nothing is impossible if you dare to dream – that is, unless you never try to make your dreams come true."

CHAPTER TWENTY-FIVE

Build It and They Will Come

With Amy at a chaperone planning meeting for Braden's upcoming trip to the Museum of Science and Industry in Chicago, Steve had taken the afternoon off to await the arrival of a new refrigerator. Their previous fridge had expired over the weekend after just five years in service.

"Don't make 'em like they used to, now, do they?" the delivery driver said. Steve had agreed and said maybe he should start a savings account to be ready for the next one. "Wouldn't hurt," the driver said. "Want me to take the box with me?"

"Leave it," Steve requested. "In case this one quits after five minutes."

"Good idea. Although they usually last at least until I get down the street." The driver's deadpan comment had Steve truly worried until the man started laughing. "Just kidding, mister. You should get good use out of this one. It's highly rated for keeping things cold and families fed."

Still, Steve kept the box just to play it safe. He moved the box to the garage and brought the two large coolers into the kitchen. "Seth!" he called, and then called out his son's name again. He knew the kid was home since he had heard his noisy used car sputter into the driveway. "Seth, come on down!"

Steve stooped over a cooler to start unpacking items that had been chilling there for when the new refrigerator arrived. When he stood back up, Seth was there. Steve jumped back, startled. Seth was already in sweats for family movie night. He was barefoot, too. "I'm going to make you wear clodhoppers so I know when you are sneaking up on me."

"Clodhoppers? What are clodhoppers?" Seth asked. "Is that some term from your childhood in the 1920s?"

"Very funny," Steve said. "Help me put these things in the new fridge."

"Shouldn't you wait for it to get cold first?"

Steve looked at his son. "Ha. Yeah, that's probably a good idea. We'll do this later." He retrieved two cans of soda from one of the coolers. "Want one?"

"Sure." Seth took his and started toward the living room, presumably to venture back upstairs.

"Wait," Steve said. "Let's sit at the table. Would you go ahead and order the pizzas? I think we know what your brother and sister want by now."

So, they sat, and Seth used his cell phone to access the pizza ordering app, adeptly navigating the world of choices pizza by pizza, topping by topping, and even selecting a delivery time. "Done," he said. "Can I go now?"

"What's your hurry? Just sit and relax. Talk to your old man. My hearing isn't so good these days, not as good as it was back in the 1920s, but give it a try."

"Whatever," Seth said.

Steve sighed and let his son's display of attitude ride for now. "Pick your battles, ol' fella," Steve told himself. "So, what's your movie choice for tonight?" he asked. "Action flick? Superheroes? Something suitable for your brother and sister, too, I hope."

Seth finished his soda in record time, belched out loud, and said, "You'll probably be surprised what movie I chose."

Steve wanted to say, "Frankly, son, nothing you do surprises me," but he simply said, "Try me," instead.

"Well, I wanted to stream that new Marvel movie, but it's got that cartoonish violence you don't think is good for Braden to see. And I sure didn't want to pick *My Little Pretty Pony Princess People* or whatever girlie stuff Abby still watches."

"Pins and needles here, Slick," Steve teased. He made a drumroll sound with his tongue."

"Alright, I'm getting there," Seth said, rolling his eyes. "I ended up picking a movie you and mom like, especially you."

"Which is…?"

"*Field of Dreams*, okay? I thought if I watched the 'origin story' of that lame quote you always say, I might not think it was so lame after all."

"You mean…."

"If you build it, they will come," Seth said.

Steve smiled. "Ah, grasshopper, 'tis true I say that often, but as you will learn, the actual quote is, 'If you build it, *he* will come'."

"Grasshopper? What'd you mean by that? Is that part of this movie, too?"

Steve laughed. "No. That's a lesson for another day. For now, I need your help with something. Your version of the *Field of Dreams* quote – which is practically everyone's version of the quote, actually – gave me an idea."

Shortly after Amy got home, the pizza delivery person arrived. She called for Braden and Abby to come downstairs and to put the puppy in the Mud Room for a while. They were slow to come. In fact, Amy found herself alone in the kitchen, alternating between putting out plates and examining the new refrigerator, still empty but cooling. It wasn't unusual for the younger kids to need multiple prompts to join the family for dinner, especially since the puppy had arrived; but it *was* unusual for Seth to need extra calls for pizza. And the fact that Steve was missing in action, too, had her concerned.

Just then, Steve and Seth came in from the garage carrying the refrigerator box. It was fully open, and they had to compress its sides slightly to get it through the door.

"Why are you bringing that in here?" Amy asked. "We really don't have room and—"

"It's not for in here," Seth said. "It's for the Family Room for family movie night."

Amy was placing slices onto plates, not really looking at the box as she spoke. "Well, I really don't think we need that in the Family Room either," she said. "Besides, the pizza's getting cold. Why on Earth would you two think it's a good idea to—" She cut herself off when she saw the box, complete with its modifications.

"Okay, that's pretty sweet," she said. "Have they seen it yet?"

"Nope," said Seth. "We've been building it on the down low."

"They're gonna love it," Amy said. "Whose idea was this?"

Steve cleared his throat. "Seth provided the inspiration and we built it together. Kind of a father and son project you might say." He winked, and Seth grinned.

Amy smiled, too. But then she cupped her hands around her mouth and yelled toward the stairs. "Kids, get down here right now. See what your father and brother built for you."

In seconds, Abby and Braden descended the stairs like a herd of buffaloes, Abby cradling the new puppy in her arms.

In unison, Steve and Seth proclaimed, "Build it and they will come."

The younger kids were delighted with what Steve and Seth had constructed. The refrigerator box was now a fanciful dugout, labeled "WHITE SOX." Strategically positioned lengthwise in the Family Room, the dugout sported large lounging pillows pilfered from the guest bedroom, an entry opening on one end and a long viewing slot along the new front. Copious amounts of duct tape fortified the dugout's corners and flaps. And along the front just below the viewing slot were three names: *Abby, Braden,* and *Toto2*.

Toto2 was the name Abby had picked out for her new dog, even though Toto2 was a fawn-colored Pug, quite unlike Dorothy's dog in *The Wizard of Oz*. Seth, of course, had scoffed at the name, saying he thought Ugly Pugly was more appropriate. Still, the teenager had also taken a shine to the pup.

Abby and Braden mostly ignored the movie, instead watching the dog sleep and giggling at his dreamy snorts. Amy watched while nestled against Steve on the couch. And Seth, after a dozen or so wistful glances in

135

the direction of the cell phone box, finally settled in and became engrossed in the movie.

Near the end of the film, Steve couldn't help but think about Vance and his admonition that Steve should focus on doing what he once loved as a means of restoring his company to greatness. The connection hit him most strongly when James Earl Jones, in the character of Terence Mann, says, *"This field, this game, is a part of our past, Ray. It reminds us of all that once was good and that could be again. Oh, people will come, Ray. People will most definitely come."* Steve now had renewed faith that by getting back to what he did best, people – *customers* – would indeed come.

"Still kinda lame," Seth said afterward, but Steve knew it was merely teenage posturing. He was surprised when Seth added, "Not as lame as I thought it would be, I guess, but, ya know."

Steve smiled. Then he walked to the front door and turned on the porch light. Looking back at his son, he said, "Wanna have a catch?"

CHAPTER TWENTY-SIX

Present in Each Moment

As he gathered work papers in his home office, Steve anticipated that this morning's meeting with Vance would be the last official session at the diner. And even though each meeting brought new "homework," Steve had come to look forward not only to the food and the fellowship at The Fork, but even to the challenges Vance presented from one week to the next.

He had worked late the night before, but now, as he collected the last of his notes to take with him, he uncovered the album he had bought at the vintage record shop – Supertramp's *Breakfast in America*. He picked it up and studied it, though his gaze quickly gave way to a rush of memories. Memories of food and coffee and aromas and pies. Memories of Jukebox Jack and Bobthecook and Vance.

And Libby.

He was admiring the album's cover art – showing the waitress in a Statue of Liberty-like pose, with a glass of orange juice on a tray in place of Lady Liberty's torch – when Amy walked in. She kissed him on the cheek and joined him in his admiration of the album art. After a moment she took it from his hands and held it at arms' length. "So," she said, "is this the other woman you've been seeing when you dash off so early to breakfast?"

"Oh no, caught in my own web," Steve joked. "How could I have been so careless?"

Amy laughed. "So, does your favorite server look like this?" she asked, and she brought the album cover closer to her eyes.

"Actually, she does a bit," Steve said. "I knew she looked familiar from the first time I visited the diner, but it took a while for me to figure out why."

"I see," Amy said, still channeling mock indignation. "So, this is your type now, huh? Maybe I should wear a uniform and that little server's cap thingy like your new lady friend here. What's her name again?" Amy leaned in even closer to the image of the server. "Ah, yes, here it is on her badge. 'Libby'. Well, 'Libby,' I want my husband back after today."

Steve looked perplexed. He took the album back from Amy and pulled it close enough to read the server's name badge. "Well, I'll be darned," he said, and then he started laughing. "I never even noticed before that Supertramp and I both have our Libby's!"

Amy smiled coyly. "You're getting old, my dear, if this is your new pin-up girl." And with that she left the room, her laughter growing as she walked down the hall.

Vance was placing the extra wire tree sculpture in a box when his wife entered the room. She pulled it back out and studied it for a moment, and then eased it back in. "I'm sure he'll love it," she said. "And how wonderful that Nancy – and Charlie, of course – made it possible for you to give it to him."

Vance smiled wistfully. "Charlie would certainly be proud of the progress Steve has made since we began this journey," he said.

She patted his arm. "Charlie would be proud of you, too."

The drive toward the diner was too quiet, with Steve's thoughts at once random and melancholy. To silence his bittersweet thoughts, he tuned the car radio to his favorite streaming music station playing classic pop hits.

Mile after mile, he sang softly along to Elton John's *Goodbye Yellow Brick Road*, Dan Fogleberg's *Run for the Roses*, and The Eagles' *The Long Run*. He tried to imagine what kinds of pies would go along with each song as it played, but ultimately decided that such pie conjuring creativity was in Libby's domain. He turned off the radio again and instantly heard Libby's voice in his head, yelling out "…B-11 and a good swift kick," thus instigating *The Logical Song* that first day.

His cell phone notification broke the quiet. A message from Amy popped up on the dashboard screen: *Center console. Thumb drive. Play it. Love you.*

Keeping his eyes on the road, Steve lifted the console cover, felt around inside, and located the thumb drive. He tried to insert it in the media slot but had it upside down at first. Once he made the connection, new music started playing; well, *old* music, actually.

The first song up was, remarkably, *The Logical Song*. He must have told Amy about that. So amazing she remembered, he thought! When that song faded, a brief pause yielded to *Shoo-fly Pie* and *Apple Pan Dowdy*. Steve laughed. Amy had remembered that one, too. And the next one and the next one and the one after that. From *Bye, Bye, Miss American Pie* to *Tin Man* to *Kung Fu Fighting* and beyond, his incredible wife had listened so closely to him and recalled with absolute clarity the smallest details of his visits to The Fork. It was a gift Amy had that he did not. He wished he could be half as *present* in each moment as she was.

Oh, how he loved that woman.

CHAPTER TWENTY-SEVEN

A New Perspective

Vance's coffee sat steaming on the corner booth table, but Vance was not seated there. Instead, he was at the opposite end of the diner chatting with Jukebox Jack. He nodded at Steve and gave him an I'll-be-there-in-a-couple-minutes gesture that told Steve his conversation with Jack was meant to be private.

Steve looked for Libby next, but she seemed to be missing in action as well. "Boss lady's not here yet," came a voice from someone who was crouched below counter level. Steve leaned forward in the direction of the voice and at that moment Bobthecook stood up and smiled. He had been placing freshly washed silverware in the tray beneath the counter.

"You startled me for a second there," Steve said.

"Sorry about that. Not used to seeing me on this side of the action, eh?"

"Well, frankly, no, but it's good to see they let you out of your cage. Good behavior?" Steve asked.

Bobthecook laughed. "Not much chance of that."

"You said the boss lady isn't here yet? You mean Libby, right?"

"Of course," said Bobthecook. "Who else?"

There was an awkward pause between the two. "So," Steve began. "Are you filling in for Libby this morning? Doing double duty?"

"Right on both counts, although she'll be in before you know it. Can I get you something in the meantime?"

"Just coffee for now, thanks. Black," Steve said.

In seconds, Libby's fill-in placed a scalding hot cup on the counter in front of Steve.

"This must not be a common thing, your stepping out of the kitchen, I mean," Steve said.

"Once in a blue moon," Bobthecook replied. "Some people do their best work behind the scenes. Guess I'm one of those people."

"Well, again, it's good to see you out front for a change. And you're certainly good at what you do," Steve said. He patted his belly. "Maybe a little too good. I'm up at least five pounds since I started coming here."

"High praise for one like me." Bobthecook beamed for a couple seconds, but then nodded over Steve's shoulder. "Here comes the boss lady now. Back to the cage!" And then, as the jangle of the cowbell subsided, Steve heard Bobthecook laugh and say, "Pay no attention to that man behind the curtain."

"Hey there, ol' buddy," Libby said, scooting past him, her arms full of paper goods for the diner. "We've been busier than usual lately, so that means we've been running through supplies quicker. Had to make a mid-week run for reinforcements."

"Good problem to have," Steve said.

"Yessiree! Not complaining." Her arms emptied, she looked Steve in the eye and said, "Coffee, black, coming right up."

"No need," Steve said. "Bobthecook took care of me. Called you the boss lady and said you let him out of his cage."

"Ha!" Libby chortled. "More likely he broke free from his chains again!"

Steve laughed. He picked up his coffee and blew on it. "By the way, now that I think about it, I don't think I've ever actually met the owner of this fine establishment. Out-of-state ownership conglomerate or something like that?"

Libby was putting away sleeves of foam cups in a cabinet, but she stopped what she was doing and turned to face Steve again. "Oh, honey, I'm sorry about that. Let me introduce you to the owner." With that, she stepped out from behind the counter, stopped next to Steve, and extended her hand.

"Hi, I'm Elizabeth. Most people call me Libby. I'm the owner and principal customer service director here at The Fork. So nice to meet you!"

Steve stood there, his jaw dropping lower with each passing second. He shook her extended hand but stammered as he tried to come to terms with his embarrassment. "I'm, I'm, well, I'm happy to finally meet you. I mean, certainly I've *met* you, but… But I guess I never really got to *know* you. And I never even suspected—"

Libby released his hand and patted him on the shoulder. "It's okay," she said. "Most people don't ask, and I don't make a point of sharing that tidbit either. I think some people might relate to me differently if they see me as something more than their friendly server at the retro diner. And when it comes right down to it, serving is what I do best. It's what I love to do, and I think that's a big part of our success." She gestured to indicate the diner and its staff and patrons inclusively.

"People get into a pretty deep focus on their own lives and their own problems and trying to find their own solutions," Libby continued. "And let's face it, I *do* play the part, and that's been a somewhat conscious decision, Steve. It's an important part of the brand, I suppose, and it does seem to work!"

"You're one smart lady," Steve said, and Libby smiled. As Steve turned to step toward the corner booth, he stopped, turned back to Libby once more, and said, "So, is it weird that I leave tips for you as the server? I mean, now that I know you own the joint it might seem awkward."

Libby reached beneath the counter and pulled out a large pickle jar, empty but for a shallow base of coins, topped by wads of mostly one- and five-dollar bills. "Community tip jar," she said. "Jenny keeps her own tips. Mine go in here and get split between Jenny and Bobthecook. Seems like the right thing."

Steve smiled and nodded. He stepped away, absent-mindedly bypassing his normal seat in the corner booth and instead taking the seat Vance normally occupies. Without realizing it, he found himself trying out a new perspective, trying to see what else he might have been missing with his back to the world inside The Fork. Ironically, he hardly noticed when Vance came up to the booth.

"I like this," Vance said. "Good to change up the view from time to time, don't you think?" He took Steve's normal seat.

Steve became aware of what he had done. "Oh, Vance, I'm sorry. I guess I'm just a bit rattled this morning. I just learned that Libby owns The Fork. I'm so ashamed of myself for not knowing that." He started to stand. "Here, let me give you back your place."

Vance waved him off. "Absolutely not. Like I said, a change of perspective is good. In fact, it's necessary from time to time." He pulled his coffee cup from in front of Steve and took a sip.

"Still—" Steve began.

"No, no, perfectly alright," Vance assured him. "We get too set in our ways, don't we? And isn't that what keeps us stuck? I suppose it made sense for a while that your primary focus was on me and the business at hand of helping turn your sales and your company around. But you've taken those lessons to heart and done so much hard work so far. It's only right and fair that you should start to expand your view."

Steve shook his head. "I suppose you're right. I guess I'm also a bit flustered because of your call a few days ago when you suggested this could be our last official session. Truth is, Vance, I've thoroughly enjoyed this experience and wish it could go on."

"And I've enjoyed it, too, Steve." Vance paused. "But as much as I'd like to see this continue as well, I think you're almost ready to leave the nest. I think the rest of it we can handle with weekly phone calls for a while. That'll save you a lot of 'windshield time' and make it possible for you to concentrate on implementing and managing the changes we've identified."

"And maybe give me time to integrate getting back to what I enjoy," Steve said.

"Absolutely," Vance affirmed. "And that's a perfect segue to our primary business discussion today. So, have you—"

Libby, ever the servant leader, stepped up. "So, have you decided what you want for breakfast?"

"Alright," Vance said, "down to business. Tell me, how did it go last week keeping track of your activities?"

Steve thumbed through his folder, pulled out the 3-column form Vance had suggested, and placed it on the table, facing Vance. "Well, I certainly found this an interesting exercise. Enlightening, you might say."

"In what way?"

Steve sighed. "In the past, I always just did the work. I just plowed ahead because things had to get done, but never really thought much about why I was doing those things or why I thought that it could only be *me* doing them – whether I wanted to or not."

"That's true of most people," Vance said. "Especially business owners who have seen their companies grow rapidly and then stall. So, what were your observations?"

Steve pulled the chart back to where both he and Vance could examine it together. "I learned a few things," he began. "I learned, or verified based on our discussion last week, that I'm doing very few things that I truly love to do. I learned that there are some activities I like to do but, in all honesty, I'm not very good at. I also learned that the activities I love to do and am good at doing, weren't even the majority of what I was dedicating my time to each week."

"Again, that's not at all uncommon," Vance said. "So, that last group of activities you mentioned – the ones you enjoy and are good at – what percentage of your time do those occupy during the week?"

Steve scanned the chart quickly. "I'd say probably twenty percent."

Vance glanced back and forth between the chart and Steve. "Okay then, so, to tie that in with what we talked about last time, what percentage would that need to be in order for you to feel like you've had a 'good week'?"

"I would say maybe sixty to seventy percent. That sounds about right."

"And what would you say if I told you it was possible to achieve that?" Vance asked.

"I'd say that would be welcome and wonderful! What would I need to do?"

"First thing to do," said Libby, placing plates on the table, is to eat and enjoy your breakfast!"

As they finished eating, Steve asked Vance, "So, can I be nosy? I noticed you were in a pretty focused conversation with Jack. I don't really know much about him either...."

"I'm sure Jack wouldn't mind me sharing with you. Most of the regulars around here know, and you're pretty much a regular at this point." Vance took a deep breath and then slowly released it. "Jack was telling me about his wishes for after he's gone. He's a sick man, Steve. Very sick. Always a quiet soul, Jack's also a Vietnam veteran, so that's made him retreat inwardly for a very long time, too."

"I'm sorry to hear that," Steve said. "My dad was a Korean War veteran, and it wasn't until his later years he started sharing memories that were too painful to talk about when he was younger. I think we knew he wasn't comfortable reliving that, so we never forced the issue. But still, it festers inside them, doesn't it?"

"We all have our internal scars, I imagine," Vance replied, "but probably none so thick and hard-earned as the scars our veterans know."

Steve was quiet, not knowing what else to say.

"Remember the Don McLean song we played some time ago?"

"You mean the one that goes 'bye, bye, Miss American Pie'?"

"Yes, that one. It has a line in there about the day the music died. Jack would like that song played one last time and then retired from the jukebox forever. And then he wants me to take over his booth when I'm here so I can play whatever song Libby calls out."

"That's a real honor that he asked you to do that, Vance."

"Yes," Vance said, and then he grew quiet for a few moments.

"Okay," Vance said. "So, let's dive into your list and see where you might be able to make some changes so you can have many better days." Vance looked at Steve's chart and then began marking it up, segmenting each activity into a "bucket." Most activities could be placed in the sales bucket, some within a marketing bucket, with most of the rest classified as "general management."

Shoving the paper closer so Steve could read his notes, he asked, "Do the results surprise you?"

"No, it's basically what I thought was the case, especially after our discussion last week. I guess I've known this for a while, but I never stopped to think about it much, let alone do something about it."

"Are you ready to do something about it now?"

"Yes sir; I can't live like this much longer."

"Okay," Vance said. "So, here's what I'd like you to consider. The 'general management' activities for the time being need to stay with you. The processes we're putting in place will help a great deal, but a COO or General Manager is not what you need your next hire to be. I know asking a former software developer to be a good marketing person is a lot to ask, but it appears not too much of your time is spent on this activity, so we could find you an outside resource to contract some of this work to."

"Okay, I agree with that," Steve said.

"Now, the elephant in the room," Vance continued, "is sales, specifically sales management. In every case, you marked that it wasn't what you loved to do, and you didn't think you were good at it. And to be honest, if the sales management activities every sales manager *should* do were on this list, your 'sales' list would be even longer."

"So, what do I do about it?"

"You hire someone to manage sales for you."

"I just don't know if I can afford that, Vance," Steve said, his face showing true concern.

"I don't know that you have any choice," Vance said. "Do you want to continue to see sales drop, be away from your family as much as you have been, *and* continue to do something you don't like to do and aren't very good at?"

"Well, when you put it that way, no, of course not."

"Then you need to start focusing on what brings you and the organization the most value."

"Which is working more with the operational and technology portions of the organization?"

"Exactly," Vance said. You'll still need to oversee other facets of the business, of course, but we need to find someone who will directly manage your company's daily activity. This will allow you to step back from deep immersion in day-to-day processes, but will still enable you to have the ultimate responsibility."

"That all makes sense."

"You see, Steve, as I mentioned before, sales managers love to do the very things you don't like to do. They've spent their entire careers honing their skills to grow sales. They love weekly one-on-one meetings, traveling with reps, coaching and strategizing on how to acquire new clients. They don't mind the hard discussions needed to hold salespeople accountable; and they love being out of the office in the field. They love every activity you don't like and aren't good at."

"I see your point."

So," Vance continued, "you need to focus on what *you're* good at and let others focus on what *they're* good at."

Steve shook his head. "I can certainly see the logic and the wisdom of that, but I also worry about cost."

"There are many different solutions that can help you still achieve the same goal. I know this to be true, because this is the world I come from and the world I'm in today. For example, you could hire a full-time VP of Sales, or you could hire what is often called a Player/Coach, or you could even outsource the sales leadership to a Fractional VP of Sales."

Vance wrote those terms on the back of the activity sheet. "Now, a full-time VP of Sales is obviously the most costly, but you would have someone to manage your team full-time," he said. "A Player/Coach, on the other hand, is someone who splits their time between the role of a Sales Leader and a Salesperson. This option is less costly than a full-time VP of Sales, but the capabilities of the person is diminished, and it can be difficult to effectively manage your time between two different roles."

"You mentioned a third option though, too," said Steve. "Is that right?"

"Yes, the third option is that of an Outsourced or Fractional VP of Sales. As the title suggests, this person functions as your VP of Sales for a 'fraction' of the time – the amount of time you need. They're not a full-time resource, but I'm not sure that you need one at this point. As you approach $16M in annual revenue, however, a full-time resource may be appropriate and necessary; and at that time, you could opt for the full-time VP of Sales."

Steve studied the titles Vance had jotted down. "I didn't realize there were so many options."

"There are," Vance said, "but of course, there are pros and cons to each option. Another thing to consider is that if you hire a full-time resource, you'll need to develop a job description, compensation plan, and a hiring plan. With an Outsourced VP of Sales, obviously, that wouldn't be necessary."

"Again, it makes perfect sense to me," he said. "Thank you, Vance."

"Sure thing. Now, give each of those options some thought, and we can connect by phone next week."

As he gathered his things to get back on the road, Libby came by. "You never asked about the pie of the day," she said.

"Oh, sorry, Libby. I've been a little off my game today, I guess. So, tell me, what is the pie of the day? I haven't really noticed any unusually delightful aromas today."

Libby handed him a card. It was a recipe.

"What's this?"

"This, my friend is what I call the 'You Can Make It if You Try Breakfast Pie.' We could make it for you, but it might not keep till you get home, and you'll enjoy it much more if you make it yourself – and make it your own way."

Steve gave her a long hug, figuring it might be a while before he would see her again. In the background he vaguely became aware of a Gospel song – *You Can Make It* – playing on the jukebox, courtesy of Jack's magic touch.

"Thank you, Libby." Steve said. "Thank you for everything."

"My pleasure," she said. "But don't thank me; thank my husband over there." She winked at Vance.

Steve's jaw dropped again, and Libby's smile grew with each passing second. "Oh, don't worry, Honey," she said. "It's kinda like me owning the diner – it's not something we make a big deal about. I know it might seem surprising; after all, Vance and I are very different kinds of people, aren't we? He's very quiet and purposeful; I'm *not so quiet*, even if I'm also purposeful. And again, both Vance and I were more concerned about your story and your business and *your* family. You've had enough on your mind trying to manage your own life without having to digest that we are married, too."

She patted Steve on the shoulder. "Let's face it, Sweetie, Vance and I are a lot to deal with as individuals – me in particular. If you had to factor in the dynamic of us as a couple… Well, your head might have exploded!"

Steve started shaking his head. "Still, I should have—"

Bobthecook rang the bell. "Order up!" And with that, Libby – Vance's wife – was off.

CHAPTER TWENTY-EIGHT

Hope Realized

After completing their last breakfast session, Steve met Vance in the parking lot. It was a beautiful day. Bright. Sunny. With a gentle breeze blowing from the west.

Steve was still shaking his head as he reached Vance. "You and Libby?" he asked. "How could I have not known you were married?"

Vance laughed. "Don't beat yourself up about it. It's not something we wave in people's faces. Don't get me wrong; I love my wife. In fact, I adore her. You could probably tell that if you looked closely enough."

"Oh, sure," Steve began. "I knew – I *know* – how fond you are of Libby. I just thought…."

"You just pictured each of us married to someone very much like ourselves, didn't you?"

"Well, sure. I guess you could say that."

"But that's pretty much impossible, don't you think?" Vance asked. "After all, opposites often attract."

Steve smiled. "Yes, I suppose that's true."

"And if we only surround ourselves with people just like us, in our personal or professional lives, how can we even hope to learn and grow?"

"Good point," Steve said. "I just still can't believe I missed this – that I couldn't have figured it out at some point. Am I that oblivious to what's going on around me? Is that part of the reason my business has been failing, too?"

Vance motioned for them to walk toward a shady spot near his car. Once there, he said, "To be honest with you, Steve, the answer to your question is 'yes,' you've been a bit oblivious. But that's not uncommon, nor is it a fatal flaw, especially if you recognize it in time. In a way, I suppose burying your head in the sand is a coping mechanism. It's simply too painful to acknowledge the truth at times, so we shut out what we don't want to see or acknowledge. Let's just say we often ignore what we're not strong enough to confront. At least for a while."

"Yes, that sounds like me."

"Oh, no," Vance said sternly, "that does *not* sound like you anymore. It sounds a bit like the old Steve, but not so much like the new and improved Steve standing before me."

"Thanks for that," Steve said, "but I'm still amazed about you and Libby. I mean, there had to have been clues – if I had been open to seeing them, of course."

"Sure, there were clues along the way," Vance said. "Those times when our cell phones would go off at the same time in a group text from our daughter, for example; or the fact that I probably mentioned my wife's name – Elizabeth – during an early discussion or two." He motioned toward the diner. "And next to the door you walked through every time you entered, is that sign that shows the name of the proprietor. While the name 'Elizabeth' might not have registered right away, the sign also shows our shared last name."

"Wow!" Steve said. "I can't believe I missed something I had to have seen many times."

"Your attention and focus were well directed elsewhere," Vance reassured him. "You were in a bit of a quandary early on. And after that, you were eager for breakfast and pie."

"And the people," Steve said. "You know, I do remember you saying once that your wife worked hard serving others in a job she loved. That certainly describes Libby." Steve laughed and looked toward the sun. "If nothing else, I guess the fact that you both had Florida tans should have told me something!"

Vance laughed, too. "Well, I hope this whole experience has been eye-opening for many reasons."

"It sure has," Steve said. After a moment, he said, "Well, I suppose I should let you get back to your life and to actual paying clients."

"Not so fast," Vance replied. "I have something for you." He walked to his car and grabbed a small box.

"What's this?"

"Well, you'll have to open it yourself to get the answer," Vance said, grinning.

Steve eased open the flap and looked inside.

"Go ahead," Vance said. "Take it out."

Steve pulled the wire tree statue from the box. For a few moments he marveled at the intricate structure, hundreds of delicate wires intertwined to form a strong trunk and its branches and limbs. The tree appeared to be caught in a storm, its branches bending together in one direction."

"I don't know what to say, Vance."

"Well," Vance began. "I've been thinking about what to say at a time like this for a while now, so let me do the honors. First of all, this was a gift from Charlie – oh, don't worry, he actually saw to it that I got *two* of these; one to keep and one to pass on. So that's what I'm doing, passing this one on to you.

"I think Charlie would say something like this: *Steve, you are like this tree. You have put down roots and you are stronger than you think. You will face many storms, but you have within you the strength and the fortitude to withstand the winds of change. To adapt. To grow. And as you grow, your view will change, your perspective will be from a higher place; and that will help you see better and reach higher still.*"

Steve struggled to smile as he brushed aside a tear.

"And if you'll look at the bottom," Vance continued, "you'll see a favorite passage of Charlie's – and mine – from a poem by Robert Browning."

Steve read the bottom of the sculpture:

Ah, but a man's reach should exceed his grasp,

Or what's a heaven for?

Vance continued: "We'll get together again soon enough, Steve. Until then, we'll keep in touch and you and your team will continue to do the hard work, I'm sure. You'll navigate the path to sales success and position your company to reach its full potential for many years to come. I have every confidence in that, and I have every confidence in *you*."

Vance shook Steve's hand, and they brought the handshake in for a brief hug.

When they separated, Vance said, "Steve, in the short time I've had the pleasure of knowing and serving you, you've gone from being hopeless to being hopeful. And now, my friend, you are well on your way to having your hope realized."

CHAPTER TWENTY-NINE

No Longer Lost

Steve was tired. Hungry, too.

But no longer lost.

It had been nearly a year since he and Vance had last met at the diner. Nearly a year since Libby had tempted him with her pies. Nearly a year since he had heard the jukebox. Tasted Bobthecook's breakfast. Sipped steaming cups of coffee.

And found himself.

As he stopped again at this familiar crossroad, The Fork looked the same as it had the first time he laid eyes upon it – aluminum skin, neon signs already lit despite the sunshine, a smattering of cars and people – and yet not the same at all. For this time he was seeing it through different eyes. He could see now that The Fork was much more than it seemed, the people inside far more than nameless, faceless souls feeding their hunger. He could see now that this was a place where hope becomes possibility and possibility becomes promise. And where promise becomes reality.

As he sat there in his idling car, the diner just before him, Steve felt a bit emotional at the prospect of the homecoming. As he had done many times in the intervening months, especially in recent days, he reflected on how much his life had changed. Since he had last met with Vance, his children had continued to mature, marking the passage of time in outgrown shoes, height marks on the kitchen door frame, a scholarship earned, and in movie nights that showed him more about his children than he could ever know by working late at the office.

His team – including Harry, Joe and Sally – had stayed on board during the often-trying times of implementing new systems and processes, and they had flourished. Where once Steve had felt completely alone in having to tackle his company's troubles, his team had stepped up and taken ownership of both problems and solutions. Because of this, Steve had been able to get back to what he was good at – providing vision and leadership for product development. And now, while his sales reps continued to outperform their quotas, Steve had been able to launch a new product, a disruptive new breed of software that had shaken up their industry and was restoring his company to a place of market leadership.

Even before the launch, however, revenue and profits had risen, thanks in large measure to the emphasis on selling the most profitable products and services to the prospects most likely to buy; but thanks, also, to more consistent, efficient and effective sales processes. As Vance had anticipated, the new CRM system was helping provide direction for this more predictable sales success.

Indeed, throughout the organization, there was confidence now. There was pride in what had been accomplished – their $16 million in annual revenue goal met and exceeded. And there was a sense of purpose.

That's what Steve would tell Vance. That's what he would share with Libby.

He would thank them again and he would commit to being present in the moment. To putting faith and family first. To keeping his eyes open to possibilities. To paying forward more than he is given. To being a servant leader.

Steve released the brake and moved the car toward The Fork.

As he parked, he could see Libby scurrying about inside. Vance's booth was empty, but when Steve looked to the opposite end of the diner, he found Vance in his new place, sitting by the jukebox, sipping coffee and ready to carry on for Jack whenever Libby would call out a song request.

Steve turned off the engine, took a deep breath and stepped from his car.

And now, as he reached the door, he saw Libby's name on the proprietor sign, just opposite the bright orange neon that still promised "Better pies, bigger pieces!"

ABOUT THE AUTHOR

Mark Thacker is President and co-founder of Sales Xceleration, a firm specializing in sales strategy, sales process and sales execution. Mark has a 30+-year history of sales leadership and success in diverse industries.

A natural leader and motivator, Mark has led sales teams with annual revenue responsibility from $1 million to in excess of $800 million. Prior to the founding of Sales Xceleration, he personally worked with over 50 companies in the small business community, serving as an Outsourced VP of Sales, helping many achieve record-breaking results. As the leader of Sales Xceleration, he has overseen the growth of over $1 billion in revenue from Sales Xceleration clients since 2011.

Mark earned his Bachelor's and Master's Degrees from Butler University, where he is a long-standing basketball season ticket holder and ardent supporter. Mark is the author of *Hope Realized: Finding the Path to Sales Success* and *Beyond the Mountaintop: Observations on Selling, Living and Achieving*, which not only recounts his trek to the summit of Mount Kilimanjaro, but highlights the sales and leadership best practices that he has learned throughout his career.

Mark and his wife, Pam, reside in Fishers, Indiana, a suburb of Indianapolis. They have been married since 1986 and have two adult children, Stefani and Kyle;, and two grandchildren, Keyden and Rio. Mark enjoys hiking, running and golfing. An Elder in his church, Mark participates on the Missions Team and leads an annual outreach event called the Day of Caring.

52227914R00093

Made in the USA
Middletown, DE
09 July 2019